D0386590

SNOW WHYTE
AND THE
QUEEN OF
MAYHEM

SNOW WHYTE
AND THE QUEEN OF MAYHEM

MELISSA LEMON

Sweetwater Books
An Imprint of Cedar Fort, Inc.
Springville, Utah

ISBN 13: 978-1-4621-1145-9

Published by Sweetwater Books, an imprint of Cedar Fort, Inc., 2373 W. 700 S., Springville, UT 84663
Distributed by Cedar Fort, Inc., www.cedarfort.com

LIBRARY OF CONGRESS CATALOGING-IN-PUBLICATION DATA

Lemon, Melissa, 1980- author.
  Snow Whyte and the Queen of Mayhem / Melissa Lemon.
    p. cm.
  ISBN 978-1-4621-1145-9
  1. Snow White (Tale)--Adaptations. 2. Queens--Fiction. I. Title.
  PS3612.E473S66 2012
  813'.6--dc23

Cover design by Brian Halley and Rebecca J. Greenwood
Cover design © 2012 by Lyle Mortimer
Edited and typeset by Joanna Barker

Printed in the United States of America

10 9 8 7 6 5 4 3 2 1

To dreams: the kind that come in the night and leave imprints on your imagination

Also by Melissa Lemon

Cinder and Ella

Many Thanks

Thanks to my publishing company, Cedar Fort, for giving me the opportunity to write this book. Whopping thanks to JoAnn Schneider, Misty Pulsipher, and Sarah Boucher for their feedback. Special thanks to Shersta Gatica for all her help. And special, special thanks to my friends and family who supported me unfathomably during the writing and editing processes. You are awesome!

Escape

This is a story about a princess, and, unfortunately, it is also about a queen. Where do I come in—a mere man without status or even means? Well, there are places along the way where I may be of importance, but for now I tell the story simply because I am the only one who can. And since this story is about a princess, we may as well begin at the start of her life.

The princess of Mayhem came into the world. What a perfectly round head—such a beauty from the first day. The king held her for the first time while the queen looked on. Some may know how a woman loses her mind after having a baby, but an evil woman—well, that is something entirely different. When the queen saw the glow in the king's eyes as he held the new babe (crying in the deafening way that babies do) she was overwhelmed with jealousy. Any love she had feigned for the child during pregnancy vanished and was replaced with hate as quickly as a candle is doused by the closing in of two fingertips.

This failed to surprise me; Queen Radiance and I had a longer history than even the royal couple. I knew her true nature. But while King Fredrick had been fooled long enough to marry the queen, his keen observation (not to mention his obvious adoration for the child) prevented the queen's feelings from going unnoticed. I watched him watching her. The queen refused to nurse the babe. In secret, she paid the baby's wet nurse double to skip feedings. And, to my astonishment and horror, the queen attempted much worse.

I listened to the conversation in the queen's private bedchamber.

"I'll be taking the baby out for a walk when her feeding is over," the queen said to the baby's nurse.

"Are you sure, Queen Radiance?" the nurse asked cagily.

"Of course I'm sure!" snapped the queen, putting on her long white gloves, a stark contrast to her dark hair and even darker eyes. "Bring her to me when you've finished."

I panicked. I couldn't think of a way to prevent the queen from taking the child out. Trapped inside my tiny prison, I paced, sweat trickling down my skin as I waited to learn what evil plans lurked inside the queen's mind.

Luckily, the king walked the garden that day. He strolled through a grove opposite the neatly trimmed waist-high hedges that grew around a large, oval garden pond. The queen entered the garden, and Fredrick caught sight of her just as she reached the edge of the water. He watched in astonishment as she bent down, letting the infant slip from her hands. The queen watched with curious eyes as the princess began to sink.

"What are you doing?" the king cried, dashing to the pond.

King Fredrick snatched the child from the water. In haste, he grabbed her ankle and yanked. The baby flailed her arms, spewing water and gasping for breath. King Fredrick placed the child over his shoulder and smacked her back over and over until a distressed but steady cry came from her mouth.

"Oh, thank heavens," said the queen, forcing a concerned look.

The king glared at her as he loosened the single button of his velvet cloak and draped it around the princess, who by now had calmed a bit.

"How dare you," the king said to his wife with a look of disgusted contempt. I'd never seen his usually pleasant face so wrinkled with anger and worry. His green eyes shone bright as he continued speaking to his wife. "I've watched you these past months—killing innocent people, your own subjects! And now this!"

"They're not actually innocent, are they? They break laws."

"The ridiculous laws you invent! You are selfish! Cruel! And mark my words, someday you'll pay for it." I could actually see spray coming from his mouth as he spat the words with gusto into her face. "Your tyranny will only bring about your destruction. And I'm not going to stand by and watch you kill my daughter." He stormed away.

"Remember, Fredrick!" the queen called, halting her husband's footsteps. "Remember that you are nothing without me. Nothing but a commoner, a servant to me and my throne. And you've seen what I do to disloyal servants."

King Fredrick swiveled to look at his dangerous and beautiful wife before carrying the child inside and arranging to sleep in the room next to the nursery.

She was, of course, correct. King Fredrick ruled merely as the husband of the queen. According to Mayhem law, one had to be a direct bloodline descendant from the previous king or queen in order to rule. Though a cousin, and her betrothed from their childhood, he could not claim legal right to the throne except as her husband, and the queen shared her power with no one—a tradition that had begun with her father, who stripped his entire family of their nobility and forced them into poverty and servitude, so that he alone had absolute power. The queen had followed in her father's footsteps, ruling cruelly and with complete domination. Despite all of this, Fredrick's fairness and kind heart earned him loyalty from many of the surrounding servants and commoners.

Late one night, after the horizon engulfed the sun's light and most of the kingdom slept, one of these servants woke the king and told him the queen's plan to send him on a hunting expedition the following day. "I believe she means to have you murdered while you are away. You . . . or the child. Perhaps even both of you."

King Fredrick threw back his covers, used the servant's candle to light his own, and went into the nursery for the babe.

"I'll need you to get me some clothes," the king whispered to the servant, gazing down on the child. "I want to look like a beggar. I want to be unrecognizable. To anyone."

"I only came to warn you," the servant said, backing away. "I can't help you escape. I'll be killed."

The king looked at the servant with pleading eyes behind the soft glow of the candle. "Only the clothes. That is all I ask. Please. For the princess."

The servant finally nodded and slipped noiselessly from the room. In his absence, King Fredrick labored to swathe the precious child without waking her. She always wore such sweet pursed lips while she slept, and her fine baby hair stuck straight up. The king quickly packed a small sack of clothing and blankets. He left so many of her beautiful things behind— gifts from the castle servants, the king's own poor relatives, and the hopeful citizens of Mayhem who counted on a new princess to someday rule their kingdom better than her mother.

The servant returned with an armful of dirty clothes from his own living quarters. "If you plan to escape tonight, you must leave now. The wet nurse will be coming soon."

King Fredrick changed his clothes, firmly clapped his hand on the faithful servant's shoulder as a grateful farewell, and picked up his darling girl, strapping her in a sturdy cloth around his neck and left shoulder. He pushed it toward his back so it appeared nothing more than the ordinary sack of a peddler.

Stepping lightly down the stone spiral staircase, the king reached the wide, arched corridor he needed to travel in order to reach the stables. Unfortunately, it also led past the servants' quarters. He glanced in every direction, focusing his attention on the door-ways that kept him hidden from nosy servants. Just as he tiptoed out into the hallway, a door creaked open. The king bowed his head and continued on, hoping to be mistaken for someone else, carrying something other than a baby. But the servant, the baby's wet nurse, eyed him carefully as she passed in the dimness.

Once out of her sight, the king ran for the door, the child bumping against his body as he moved. Outside the castle the wind lashed, a storm brewing all around. The king hurried across the rocky path that led to the stable entrance, his stringy, light brown hair dancing wildly in the wind. Though not as grand as Mayhem's castle, the stables made an extravagant home for the animals. A great, open hall spread to his left and right, connecting to each animal's stall. Fredrick rushed to the third stall on his right side and mounted a gray gelding, the queen's own coveted horse. It is the animal I would have chosen as well; his speed was famed throughout all of Mayhem and beyond.

The horse bolted down the stable hall, out the open doorway, and across the countless tiny rocks that created weaving paths around the castle. They streaked through the garden, catching the attention of several bewildered guards, but pressed on, leaving the castle grounds without a challenge.

By this time, the wet nurse knew full well what had happened.

"Your Loveliness!" she exclaimed in breathless panic as she burst through the queen's door. The queen slept in her own private bedchamber in a solitary part of the castle; she valued her privacy above all else, and the woman had run a great distance to find her.

"What?" the queen snapped, sitting up and yanking off her sleeping mask, the force of which simultaneously released a few curls from the long, loose braid she wore every night.

"King Fredrick and the princess . . . they're gone."

Even before she got to her window, her husband and daughter had left the road altogether and entered Fluttering Forest, the expanse of rugged terrain separating the queen from her greatest enemies, the neighboring kingdom of Mischief.

The queen stomped about the castle in her thin, black silk nightgown, white velvet robe, and deer skin slippers. She reached the castle gate just after two of the guards from the garden, who were already giving their report to the gatekeeper.

"What happened?" she demanded.

"He escaped through the back garden gate," one of the guards said. "We had no notice, no time to stop him."

"And he rode out on your horse," the other said.

The queen lowered her eyelids slowly until her lush, black lashes brushed across her cheeks. I knew the meaning of that particular gesture. They would lose their lives, but the queen had to keep calm long enough to take care of the more pressing situation. She dismissed the guards in order to speak privately with the gatekeeper, who doubled as Mayhem's executioner.

"What would you have me do, Your Loveliness?"

"Find them. And kill them both."

It never ceased to amaze me how cool and unfeeling she could be, even when sentencing someone to death. She whirled around, returning to her bedchamber where she would wait to learn the fate of her family and to plan the beheadings of her inattentive guards. Perhaps they should not have told her about the horse.

The moon glistened—bright and full—and King Fredrick frantically rode deeper and deeper into the forest, away from the royal castle of Mayhem, and toward the neighboring kingdom of Mischief.

His first and only clue someone followed came in the form of an uneasy horse. Several miles into the forest, after the horse had stopped to rest, the gray gelding began resisting Fredrick's commands and jerking his head one way or the other. I bit each of my fingernails down to the flesh as I watched in agonizing suspense. He needed the animal's cooperation if he hoped to escape. The executioner was on his trail, having released the king's bloodhounds to join in the search.

"Easy, boy," the king whispered roughly, then followed with several kicks to the horse's belly. "Ya!

Ya!" The steed bolted ahead, letting out a cry of unwilling submission.

Wind howled all around them, muffling the sound of the horse's pounding hooves. King Fredrick switched directions, taking a back trail toward the western outskirts of Mischief, while his pursuer stuck close to the road winding through the forest. It would lead to the heart of Mischief and, eventually, its royal castle. Taking this into consideration, combined with the weather and Fredrick's lead, the executioner had little hope of finding the king, even with the dogs. I breathed a sigh of relief.

King Fredrick rode mercilessly, stopping to let the horse rest for less than a quarter of every hour. They pressed on throughout the whole of the night and into dawn, sunrise, and full heat of day. Finally, the king reined in his horse and paused for a moment at the edge of a broad, mountainous orchard that spanned nearly a square mile. Its beauty slowed my heart; never before had I seen such open, flourishing, and green land. I longed to be there, free from the walls that surrounded me, free to take care of the princess. I would have loved nothing more.

Soft, muffled cries came from the princess's mouth, but the king offered nothing for her to eat. While permitting the animal to catch his breath, the king watched and listened closely for oncoming horse hooves. Other than the babe and the heavy wheezing of the horse, a warm stillness covered earth and sky; even the wind rested.

"We're almost there, boy," the king muttered, adjusting his position as well as the princess's. How uncomfortable they looked; my own legs ached, though I had only watched Fredrick ride for so long. "Just a little farther. Ya!" he yelled, whipping the reigns against the horse and sticking his boot into the gelding's gut.

They reached a lone, crooked house on the far end of the orchard. Fredrick slid off the horse, carefully cradling the babe, and began a weary, awkward run toward the home. He pounded his fist on the knotty birch wood door, waiting restlessly for someone to answer.

I wondered who the house belonged to, knowing the king's closest family members—once nobility and now impoverished—still resided in Mayhem. The door creaked open to reveal a white-haired, jovial sort of man.

"Can I help you?" The man smiled as he spoke, but his lips soon straightened. "Fredrick? Is that you?"

"Hello, Uncle Barney." The king gave a slight smile. It comforted me, witnessing the king's reaction to his pleasant and kind-looking uncle.

"Fredrick, I heard you married the queen of Mayhem some time ago. Whatever on earth are you doing here?" The old man's eyes fixed on the bundle in the king's arms as it let out a soft cry. "And what is it that you've got there?"

King Fredrick peeled the wrappings off the babe and lifted her out of the cloth sling. "This is the princess of Mayhem."

Fondness and apprehension mingled in the aging man's eyes. "Surely you did not come all the way here to show me your new child."

"No, Uncle. I need you to take her. I am sorry to be placing this burden on you, but our lives are in danger."

Barney pulled Fredrick inside the house and closed the door. "Then you must both stay."

"No, I cannot. Please take her. I must go. I must get far away from here. Please take her. Please take care of her." Frantic, the king forced the child into the old man's arms. She wailed her disapproval. Fredrick looked around for a moment, taking in the open room furnished with a desk, chair, and an untidy bed that sat beneath a window. On one side of the room, a wall separated them from the kitchen, and on the other, a fireplace sat beside a narrow staircase that led to an upper room.

The man held fast to the infant, a dazed look on his face, and managed to stutter a response. "But . . . but where are you going?"

"Keep her safe. I'm counting on you, Uncle." His words grew even more earnest. "Do you understand?"

His uncle nodded.

"Her name is Kat—" The king stopped suddenly and motioned for Barney to be silent by drawing a long finger to his lips. "Do you have animals?" he whispered. "I thought I heard something. I believe we were followed, but I thought I'd lost them long ago."

He had lost them, but I had no way of letting Fredrick know that. I hated to think of him leaving the child. I hated to think of what would happen to him if the queen's executioner found him. I couldn't bear the thought of having to see the princess dead.

"I have several animals." Barney steadied the baby in one arm so he could point toward the kitchen. "They're out in the barn behind the house."

The king walked through the doorway that led into the kitchen and to the tattered side window that overlooked the barn. Before the old man could ask another question, before the princess even received a kiss good bye, the king retraced his steps, sending only a regretful glance to the bundle in Barney's arms. With giant tears forming in his small, green eyes, King Fredrick hasted out the door, onto the horse, and away.

Nightfall approached as the king rode in no particular direction. It didn't matter where he went from his uncle's house, as long as he headed away from the princess and away from the queen.

Once a great distance from Barney's house, Fredrick

stopped at a stream to let the horse drink and rest. While the gelding stretched its neck toward the steady trickle of flowing water, a loud snapping sound came from behind Fredrick. He swirled around, and where before nothing but trees inhabited, a band of robbers stood ready to close in on him.

"We'll be taking whatever riches you're hiding there." The cloth in which the princess had been wrapped still hung from the king's neck.

"I don't have anything but the clothes you see on my body and the horse beneath," the king said, raising his hands in surrender.

Nearer they came, from every direction now, closing their circle to surround the king.

"Then we'll be taking the clothes and the horse," another robber said, leering.

One bandit shoved Fredrick from behind. Another pulled the horse away from him. Fredrick tried to rise to his feet, but the boot of yet another man caught him in the gut. Loud ripping sounds tore through the air as they rent his clothes, their laughter ringing out into the dusk. I will spare you the remainder of the bloody details, other than this: before dark, the king's body became a feast to a pack of ravenous wolves. I couldn't watch, knowing he'd sacrificed so much, wondering if the princess of Mayhem would ever know he'd given his life to save her.

King Fredrick's death would give the kingdom

reason to mourn, but perhaps it was a lucky misfortune. Three days later, the queen's executioner happened upon the same stream. As he came upon the gore, he covered his nose and used the boot on his foot to inspect. Though Fredrick's distorted body was beginning to decay, enough of his kind, genteel face, including his small features and green eyes, provided identification. The executioner reached down for something. A bloody cloth—empty and torn—remained strapped around the king's neck.

He began his journey back to the castle, but the queen did not wait for him to return. She asked me to show her the king, and I obliged.

Living inside a small, magical mirror—a prisoner to Queen Radiance—I thought of King Fredrick. The image of his body appeared in the mirror for the queen to see—dried blood, surrounding forest. A screeching vulture landed in that moment to grab for final pickings. Its image is forever framed in my remembrance, for the queen and I saw the exact same thing when we looked through the surface of the mirror: oval glass, braided gold decorative trim, and a faded view of each other behind it all. I could barely see my own reflection with everything else before me; I looked tired, and needed a shave. I hoped she would not ask me specifically to show her the princess, knowing she lived and breathed and drank goat's milk from a bottle.

"Are you sure it's him?" she asked. The queen of

Mayhem did not shudder or even flinch, which filled me with anger.

I narrowed in on Fredrick's still eyes to answer, showing her the lifeless result of her cruel ways.

"And the princess?"

"She is gone as well."

"Killed?"

I gave a yawn for added measure; I didn't want to let her know I cared. "Eaten by wolves. I saw the whole thing."

"Where were they?" she asked.

"In the forest beyond Mischief."

"That worthless executioner."

"If it's any consolation, he did find them," I reported. "He's on his way back to Mayhem as we speak."

Now, there's one thing you need to know. The queen thought I did not have the ability to lie to her. When she cast the spell that locked me in the mirror, she attempted to require my truthfulness. But what the queen did not know is that spells are funny things. They choose carefully which words to obey and which to cast off to the wind. When a spell is born, it selects its own characteristics. I had learned over the years that I could lie to her—I lied almost every time I told her she looked beautiful—but it didn't matter; she trusted no one, and almost always asked me to prove what I said. So when I lied, as I had just done about the princess, I always followed up with a bit of the truth, to serve as a hopeful distraction that would keep her from learning the secrets I kept. But this time, she soaked up every word. Her executioner would even live to take another life.

"And Jeffry?" she inquired. That was the name of her horse.

"Stolen."

"Poor Jeffry," she cried, slumping onto the cushioned bench in front of her vanity and producing a flow of tears. I resided inside the hand mirror atop the polished chestnut vanity, and watched as her tears descended toward me, some splashing against the mirror's frame, some acting like tiny sprinkles of rain inside my prison cell. I hated that she showed such feeling for an animal and cared nothing about her own daughter and dead husband. I glared at her as she covered her eyes and sobbed. Only a moment later, she switched off her tears, stood up from her bench, and called for a servant to draw her bath.

A heart-wrenching sorrow came over me, and anger swelled inside me; I wanted to spit in her face. I could see everything whilst inside the mirror, for that is its magic charm. But being stuck inside the mirror was a curse put upon me by the queen herself, a way to entrap me in her servitude forever. I hated the queen of Mayhem, and when I saw what she did to her own daughter, and how the king of Mayhem

died to save the princess, I chanted a spell for the first
time in ages. I had stopped trying to create spells to
get me out of the mirror; nothing had worked so far.
And my limited strength prevented me from attempting spells for anything else. But the princess needed
protection, and I was desperate to help her. The words
came directly from my heart, slow and low; I uttered
them with great feeling.

> "Winter wind chilling
> Frightening and thrilling
> Place your veil with care.
>
> Mayhem's queen reigns
> Severe and insane
> A challenge, if you dare:
>
> The kingdom's lone daughter
> Avoided death's slaughter
> But may again need grace.
>
> If danger should find her
> Let it not bind her
> With snow, cover her face."

I felt cold after; a cool breeze came inside my stag-
nant existence and swept across my face, forcing a
shuddering chill. I hoped that meant my spell was

taking life—that despite being trapped, despite my lack of strength and practice, despite the fact that the queen's superior powers held me bound, I could still create a spell to save the princess. A spell that would actually work. And from that day forward, I kept watch over the beloved child, the princess of Mayhem, whose name was Katiyana. In the language of the forefathers of Mayhem, it means . . . Snow.

Blindness

It is a strange thing, being a part of so many lives while being apart from them. I've watched many lives over the years, but none so frequently as Katiyana. I knew her perhaps even better than she knew herself. I didn't mind her ignorance of me, but I hoped that someday we would meet face to out-of-mirror face. And I always watched her with great care, cautious not to raise any suspicion in Queen Radiance. Keeping the princess a secret was vital to her safety.

Barney filled his role well. He fed the princess, changed the princess, and bathed the princess.

"Dear little one," he said as he rocked her in the chair he had made with his own hands just days after she first came. I believed he adored the princess's company, small as it was. How he rambled on. "Kat is no name for a little girl, but that is what your father called you, so it will have to do. And my family name is Whyte, the same as your father's mother. So we will call you Whyte as well. Kat Whyte. There, it suits you."

Although Barney may have called her Kat, and indeed she grew up knowing no other name, in my mind I preferred to call her by her full name, Katiyana. I never forgot her true identity, that she was the princess of Mayhem.

He introduced her to the animals before she could walk. Her first word was a shaky "Baaaaaaaaa." She began learning milking techniques soon after that. Such a bright thing!

Katiyana toddled after Barney as he walked about the orchard preparing for the fall harvest. But when it came time to take the apples to market, Barney remembered his duty to King Fredrick. "You can't come with me, Kat."

As an infant, she had waited in her little basket at the foot of Barney's bed. The closest window looked out the back of the house onto much of the orchard, but Katiyana didn't know that. She played with her toes, cooed to herself, and sucked at the bottle Barney had left close by.

A walking toddler caused a bit more of a stir, and the year after Katiyana had come to him, Barney came home from the market several times to tipped-over chairs, crumbs all over the table and floor, and blankets and pillows spread about the house.

By the time Katiyana turned four years old, Barney moved her to the tiny upstairs room where she slept on a lumpy mattress under an intricate but faded quilt. She began to protest when Barney left her alone while he went to the market. "Why can't I come?" she asked with pouted lips, standing beside the rocking chair. Babyhood lingered in her pudgy fingers and facial features. Her hair had grown so long already, and dark like her mother's, though not as coiled. But unlike her mother, she had soft blue eyes.

"Now don't fret, Kat." Barney knelt in front of her, peering into her eyes, his shirt coming untucked in the back as it always did. "You know you can't come to the market with me. If you come with me, who will look after the orchard? I need you to stay here."

"But, Uncle, you need me to go with you. I could help steer the cart. Or I could watch the apples while you try to sell them. Or I could just stay hidden and look at everything from under a blanket." She spoke so eloquently for a child, a credit to her uncle. I wondered if he'd been considered nobility at one point, like Fredrick.

"I'm so sorry, Kat. I know you only want to help your old uncle, but I will not budge. Not this time. Not when it comes to the market. I need you to stay here and take care of the orchard."

She bowed her head. "Okay, Uncle." Then she wrapped her arms around his neck. "I love you," she said.

Barney returned her hug and patted her on the head. He chuckled softly. "I love you too, my little kitten." He stood up in preparation to leave. "Be a good girl," he said, pointing straight at the princess's nose.

"I will," she said back. She swayed back and forth with her hands clasped behind her back as she watched Barney turn to leave.

And she kept her word. Katiyana went out to the barn and pulled down a pruning saw. I cringed, worried she might cut herself on its long, sharp teeth, but she dropped it on top of the hay-covered ground without a scratch. She hefted the ladder and looked up as it came crashing down. I covered my eyes, afraid the weight would crush her, but worrying for such a capable little girl proved folly. She got out of the way just in time for it to slam on top of the saw. Still carefree and confident, Katiyana dragged both to the nearest apple tree with great difficulty. She even scraped up her legs in the process, but refrained from crying or complaining. Such a determined thing!

Barney came home to find a clean house this time—completely untouched. "Kat, I'm home," he called out after tying up the tired horse and walking up the steps to the house. He opened the creaking door and his eyes took in the stillness and cleanliness before him. The setting sun provided little light, but he immediately noticed Katiyana wasn't in sight.

Barney searched under his bed and in the kitchen. "Are you hiding?" he sang playfully as he crept about. (I must say, playing Hide and Seek is no fun when you live inside a mirror and know where everyone is.) After finding her room empty, his search took him outdoors. "Kat!" he called again and again, but he could not see the child. "Oh, forgive me Fredrick," he muttered. Then, as he passed the barn, he saw the ladder underneath a tree; a little body lay at its side. "Kat?"

It did no good to call her name. Princess Katiyana had worn herself out trying to get the ladder set up and would not wake. Barney lifted her sweaty body into his arms with a broad smile on his face. "Don't worry," he whispered. "You'll know everything about taking care of an orchard in no time."

And his prophecy became reality. At age five she picked her first barrel of apples.

"Careful up the ladder now," Barney said. "Steady."

But while her uncle worried, Katiyana marched up the ladder as if she'd done it a thousand times before. At age six she pruned her first tree. And at age seven, Barney began teaching her to read letters and numbers, soon giving her charge of recording their harvest, earnings, and expenses.

Year after year she begged to go to the market, giving reasons upon reasons, such as needing a new dress and not trusting Barney to choose the right color or size. Barney Whyte remained steadfast, refusing to let the child venture outside the orchard. "I know you wanted to come to the market with me, Kat. But I've brought you something," Barney persuaded as he waved a story book in front of the princess, who sat in the corner sulking.

Katiyana looked up at him. "What's that?"

"It's a book."

"I've seen a book before," Katiyana said. "You've got seven of them on your desk."

"Not like this one. Those are for keeping records so I know how many apples we collect and sell each year. This one is especially for little girls." He opened it and Katiyana lifted her chin further. "It has pictures. And a story, like the ones I tell you at bedtime."

"But your stories never make any sense." She folded her arms in a huff and scowled.

"It has pictures," he sang.

Katiyana got up on her knees for a better view as Barney approached. He sat in the rocking chair and beckoned her to climb on his lap. Together, they read a fine tale about a milk maiden who dreamed of traveling to the stars.

From then on Barney could not keep enough books in the house. Katiyana began writing the stories herself; she even drew the pictures. But the books Barney brought were her favorites. They were, after all, her only view of anything other than life on an apple orchard.

What an irony—that I had a view of everything, and she had a view of almost nothing. I engaged myself in her life, eager to see what would happen to her. Would she remain with Barney forever? Would the queen ever discover her? Would she stay happy?

I took great delight in watching her grow. Such a happy thing—never complaining. And she really could talk Barney into anything, even picnics atop the roof on summer afternoons.

The only thing her charming manipulation did not work for was her strong desire to go to the market each fall. Every year she begged, reasoned, and bribed with the promise of doing extra chores or baking a sugar cake. On this, however, Barney always remained firm. Fredrick truly had chosen wisely in trusting Katiyana to his tender care.

When Katiyana was eleven years old, she woke one foggy winter morning, lingered in the warmth of her covers for a time with a book, and then sped down the stairs in time to feed the animals. Barney lay in bed.

"Uncle? Are you still sleeping?"

He breathed in a quick breath and let it out slow.

Katiyana reached out her arm and softly touched his shoulder. "Uncle?"

Barney jerked and opened his eyes, propping himself up on one elbow. He blinked once and then again.

"Are you all right, Uncle?" she asked. "I'm just going out to feed the animals. Would you like me to make you some breakfast first?"

"No, no, I'll be fine."

Katiyana hesitated, observing her uncle for another moment before looping the handle of a basket around her arm and walking out the door.

Barney tried to get up, using his arms to feel the air all around him. When Katiyana returned, he still sat on his bed.

"Uncle, are you sure you're well? Maybe you've got a cold." She took off her brown, fuzzy knitted gloves and placed them on the table. Then she began putting wood in the fireplace.

"I'm blind," he said softly.

Katiyana walked over to her uncle and grasped his hand, holding onto it as she pulled it up to the height of her waist. "What did you say? Are you not feeling well?" She stooped slightly to look into his face.

"I'm blind."

"I'm sure you just need some more rest," she said, shaking her head. She began patting his pillow and pushing on his shoulder. "Lie down and close your eyes."

Barney jerked away from her. He pushed against

the bed, finally rising to his feet, and tottered toward the door, constantly checking his balance. He tripped on a crack in a floorboard and nearly fell forward into the rocking chair before correcting his balance. Katiyana tried to steer him, but he only pushed her away.

Barney stumbled down the porch steps and to the barn. He felt for the horse and mounted it bareback.

"Uncle, where are you going?"

"To the market," he grunted. "Stay here."

"Let me go with you," Katiyana demanded. "You can't go alone. How will you get there?"

"I'll manage!" A look of guilt crossed his face at hearing Katiyana's silence after that. "The horse knows the way," he said kindly, leaning slightly in her direction. "We'll be all right."

Katiyana watched them ride away, lingering outside the barn, the wind swaying the skirt of her dress. Storm clouds began to gather, blocking out the sun's light. I wanted to put my arm around her—tell her everything would be all right. But I could do nothing, and Katiyana went inside the house alone. She spent the rest of the day absently poking at the smoky fire and pacing in a circular motion from the kitchen door to the staircase and back again, looking out each window as she passed. Gentle rain fell sporadically throughout the day. How I longed to smell it. How I longed to be there with her, to keep her company, to comfort her.

Nightfall arrived before Barney did. Katiyana heard the horse return and ran outside to greet them. At first, she stood there, looking expectantly at her uncle for an explanation.

"I'm tired, Kat," he said, letting out a long, heavy sigh.

"Come inside, Uncle." Katiyana reached up to help Barney down from the horse, but he slid off and into her arms, the weight of his body crashing down on her. They landed in a pronounced heap, the hay rustling beneath them. With Kat's help, Barney rolled off of her, and Katiyana moaned, holding a sore spot on her side. She struggled to get to her knees, her hair now jumbled with straw. Barney remained on his back, his shirt untucked all the way around, a bottle of ale clasped firmly in his hands, his wispy white hair standing upright. Katiyana finally stood, helping him to his feet and then gently pushing him to a sitting position atop an upside-down crate.

"What happened?" Katiyana asked, pulling the horse into his stall. "Why did you go to the market?"

"I . . ." he began breathlessly, as if he had done the running instead of the horse. "I needed to get help. For the orchard. I've hired someone to come every day."

"I can take care of the orchard myself," Katiyana responded. "I don't need any help."

"No," he said back. "You can't go to the market. I can't let you leave this orchard."

"But why, Uncle?"

"Because nobody can know about you."

Katiyana pouted and crossed her arms. "What about the person you hired? Am I supposed to hide from him? What about all these years you've gone to the market and purchased dresses and storybooks for a little girl? Have you told no one about me?" She lowered her eyes. "Are you ashamed of me?"

Barney lifted his hand and used his fingers to motion her toward him. "Come here, Kat, darling."

She knelt in front of him and his hands wandered for her face. "Listen to me," he said calmly. "You don't have to hide, not on the orchard. I only purchase things for you from people who don't know me or where I live. I'm trying to keep you safe."

"Safe from what?"

Another heavy sigh came from his lips as he hung his head. He thought for a moment before lifting his chin once more. "I've said too much already. Please trust me, Kat. That is all I ask. And as for the boy I've hired, he's a scrawny, uneducated lad who won't know the difference between you and one of his fifteen sisters." He scoffed at the idea. "He's a Simkins, Kat. You'll have to help him. I'll be surprised if he even knows how to read."

His face softened. "But above all, I need you to stay here at the orchard. People would wonder where you'd come from. I've never told anyone about you, dear one, but it's not because I'm ashamed."

"Why then? Where did I come from?" Katiyana asked. It hadn't been the first time. "Why won't you tell me why I can't leave the orchard?"

"It's just not safe," he said.

Perhaps Katiyana wondered if it wasn't safe for her or if it just wasn't safe at all; plenty of the stories she read talked of danger and harmful people. But they were also filled with heroes and heroines who thwarted them. Nonetheless, whatever confusion Barney caused, however unsatisfactory his answers, Katiyana's questions ceased.

"C'mon, Uncle. Let's get you inside." She gently lifted his left arm and helped pull him to his feet. "What's in the bottle?"

"Oh, just a little something to numb things up for a bit," he said with a smile. "That Simkins boy comes early tomorrow, so let's make sure everything's ready."

Katiyana hooked her arm with Barney's as they walked up the steps and to the table. Under a cream-colored linen cloth sat a slice of freshly baked bread and a bowl of horseradish and onion soup. The tiny white flowers from the horseradish plant stemmed from a glass bottle, resting unevenly between two slats of the pine table. Once seated (with Katiyana's help), Barney swayed his fingers over the meal, attempting to find the spoon, but ended up with his fingers in the soup. Katiyana retrieved a nearby napkin.

"Let me help you," Katiyana said, wiping his hands clean and then preparing a spoonful of broth.

Barney reached for the spoon and grabbed it away from her, nearly striking himself in the shoulder. "I don't need your help!"

Katiyana looked him over, bemusement emanating from her blue eyes and crinkled brow. "Why won't you let me help you?"

"I won't have it!" He tried looking toward Katiyana, but missed by several inches and stared into nothing. "I won't have you feeding me or treating me like a baby."

A ghostly silence crept into the house after that.

Barney gripped his spoon anew, used his opposite hand to feel around for the edge of the bowl, and went at it again. And other than a few dribbles that slid down his chin and back into the bowl, he succeeded. "I'll need you to help with the orchard, just as you've always done."

Katiyana nodded. "Of course I will, Uncle."

"You'll have to teach the Simkins boy. I'm sure he knows about nothing except getting into trouble." He dropped his spoon and rubbed his head, his elbow resting on the table.

"I'm sure everything will be fine," Katiyana said. "Why are you so upset?"

He tried once again to direct his eyes at her and failed. "My father went blind, and his father before him. I hoped my whole life it wouldn't happen to me. And now it has." His fingertips reached out over his bowl to the bottle of ale resting on the other side of his dinner. He knocked it over, but Katiyana caught it deftly and slid it into his waiting hand.

Barney wiped away a tear and stood from the table. Walking across the wood floor, he tripped twice before falling at last into the rocking chair. The chair he had rocked Katiyana in for so many years became the chair he would rock himself in. "The boy comes in the morning," he said. "Try to get some sleep."

Katiyana watched him open the bottle and take a drink. She went to him, leaned forward, and kissed his cheek, grimacing when the strong smell of liquor reached her nose. "I love you, Uncle," she said.

Barney did not answer.

Katiyana marched up the stairs to her tiny room at the top. Only a bed fit in the small space, with minimal walking room around two of its sides, and a little square window overlooked the damp orchard. She stared at the walls for a time—her thoughts deep—before lying on her pillow to cry.

Watching Barney lose his sight put my position into perspective. While I saw entirely too much, he would never see again. I ached considering how much it must have hurt the princess, and waited eagerly for the morning, wondering who would come, and what it really meant to be a Simkins, for I had never before heard such a name.

Jeremy Simkins

This may be a good place to tell you about sleeping inside the mirror. I longed for a good night's sleep! The space inside the mirror fit only a chair. I could stand or sit or even lie down if I stuck my head under the chair, but most of the time when I needed to sleep, I sat in the chair and rested my head against one of the walls surrounding me. How my bottom ached at times! So while I'd like to say I rested well that night, I can't. And neither did Katiyana. She tossed and turned, finally getting out of bed with only a hint of sunshine coming through the window. She stretched and yawned and rubbed her sleepy eyes, abandoning her morning ritual of reading before rising.

The princess wore her usual clothing, a simple

calf-length dress that fit a bit loosely on her slender frame. Money from the orchard could not buy the luxuries of brand-new dresses, especially those of bright colors. In fact, Barney most often brought clothing that others had thrown out. She had two dresses made of coarse wool for the winter time, one the color of mud and the other the dark gray of storm clouds, and two linen dresses to wear in warmer weather, although both were the exact same design and color—that of dead grass—so I could not tell one from the other. She looked the same day after day. Once, Barney had splurged on some material that captured and accentuated the blue in her eyes. Using a picture in one of her books as a guide, Katiyana made an apron with a pocket, which came in handy working in the kitchen or out on the orchard; many apples spent long afternoons in her apron pocket.

Barney waited at the table when Katiyana entered, sipping a steaming cup of tea. He'd managed well on his second day of blindness.

"He's coming," Katiyana said, looking out the kitchen window that faced the barn.

"Well, I'll be burnt toast," Barney said as he carefully set down his cup. He turned toward the side of the house, as if to look out the window. "He's on time. Fix us some breakfast, Kat."

A cauldron of water hung over the kitchen fire. Katiyana used a paddle to slide a loaf of yesterday's bread back in the brick oven. Just as she pulled the paddle out, a knock sounded at the door, jolting the princess. She jumped backward and looked anxiously at her uncle. And who can blame her? She'd never heard a knock at the door before.

"Well, open the door for him, Kat."

She hesitantly inched her way toward the door, opening it slightly to look at the person on the other side. I wanted to laugh at the boy come to save Katiyana from having to do the work herself. Everything about him screamed puny—little blue eyes, a little mouth and nose, short hair, small hands, skinny legs and arms. Katiyana was even taller than him, and thicker too, which I thought impossible.

The princess opened the door wide for the boy; he looked to be about her same age, maybe a year or two older.

"Come in here, boy," Barney called.

Katiyana clasped her hands behind her back as she led the boy through the kitchen doorway. She busied herself with retrieving the bread from of the oven and pouring a fresh cup of tea. The boy stood in front of Barney with a sort of confident air; he held his head high, his shoulders square, and actually looked happy to be there.

"What's your name?" Barney asked, his eyes directed at the boy's shoulder.

"Jeremy Simkins," he said, and although

everything else about him was small, his voice was not; he spoke loud and clear.

"What do you think, Kat?" Barney asked, turning his head toward the oven. His eyes aimed more toward the ceiling now. "Does he look like he can work?"

Katiyana looked the boy over and shrugged to herself. She placed a slice of warm buttered bread in front of Barney and grabbed his hand, pulling it up to touch the bread so he knew where to find it. "I don't know, Uncle. Not particularly sturdy, I guess."

"Thank you for the warm bread, Kat. And sturdy or not, he'll have to do." He rotated his head slightly, attempting to look in Jeremy's direction now. "I'm Barney Whyte. You may call me Mr. Whyte or sir, whichever suits. And this is my niece, Kat. She's going to teach you what to do. Winter's coming to an end. The trees need to be pruned before things begin to thaw and buds grow."

"Yes, sir," Jeremy said before following Katiyana outside.

"So he's your uncle?" Jeremy asked just as they reached the barn.

Katiyana lifted the pruning saws off the hooks and placed them outside the barn.

"Where are your parents?"

Katiyana hefted the tall ladder and stood it in front of Jeremy, leaning it forward until he took it. She looked him in the eye as he continued his questions.

"How long have you been taking care of this orchard? Is it hard to take care of apple trees? Don't they just grow on their own? Do you know how to talk?"

I'd never seen her so expressionless and wondered how she felt about being exposed to a strange boy, especially such a talkative one. She went back in the barn for the shorter ladder.

"Kat," he said, still holding up the wooden ladder that towered over him. "Maybe you don't speak words. Meow," he said, as if asking her a question in cat talk. "Meow, meow, meow, meow-meow?" He laughed at his joke. "And it's Kat Whyte? Why not Kat Black or Kat Yellow?"

Katiyana shoved the second ladder against the first, the collision nearly knocking Jeremy over. With bright red cheeks, she ran away from him and into the house.

"What's the matter?" Barney asked when she entered. "Has he done something already?"

Katiyana cried silently as she stood in front of the table and poured another cup of tea for her uncle. "No, Uncle."

"What's the matter then?"

"I just don't like him."

"Well, he's a Simkins—nobody likes him." His eyes were directed just to the side of his niece. "But we need him."

Katiyana slid the tea in front of her uncle. Barney held out both hands toward her, and Katiyana shifted slightly until his hands rested on her arms. Her lips quivered, but she remained quiet. "Give it time. Maybe he's not so bad. Maybe you'll be friends. I haven't seen you cry since you were a baby. Are you sure you're all right?"

"I'll be fine, Uncle." She wiped her tears. "Drink your tea."

Katiyana left the house and returned to Jeremy, who by now had already set up both ladders in the orchard. He was climbing up the ladder holding a saw in his hand

"No, don't do that," she said, running after him. "Hand it to me. I'll show you."

She displayed how to climb the ladder with the saw hanging on one end of the log steps. "Never climb with the saw in your hands. Rest it here or let me hand it to you when you're up."

"Why?" Jeremy asked.

Katiyana thought for a moment. "I don't know," she said. "That's just how my uncle taught me to do it."

"Maybe it's in case I fall. Landing on a saw doesn't sound like fun."

Katiyana nodded. "That makes sense." They exchanged places again and Katiyana held the saw while he climbed.

"Why is my uncle so unnerved by your being a Simkins?" she asked.

The question froze Jeremy, his right leg just reaching the fourth step. He turned to face her. "So I can't make fun of your name, but you can make fun of mine?"

"I wasn't making fun," Katiyana said. "I only asked a question."

"How about I don't make fun of you anymore and you don't ask any questions about my name?" He held out his hand.

Katiyana looked at his smooth, clean hand. She glanced down at her own—rough, calloused, and dirt-stained. The contrast amazed me; it appeared the boy had never worked a day in his life. Jeremy's eyes remained steady on hers until she accepted his flawless, outstretched hand.

Over the next few days, the two formed a routine: Jeremy came, they fed the animals, pruned apple trees, ate lunch with Barney, pruned more apple trees, fed the animals, and said good-bye.

Time flitted by. Day after day, year after year, they worked side by side—pruning apple trees that dotted a rocky expanse of land before spring; harvesting in the fall; sweltering in the summer heat as they cut back the fruit of overburdened branches; breathing out white puffs of air in the winter as they cared for the animals and waited for spring.

The children grew; Katiyana filled out some, transforming into the most beautiful, dark-haired girl I'd ever seen, with bright, eager eyes and even, olive-toned skin. Jeremy passed Katiyana in height and size within a couple of years and now stood a fine-looking, strong young man. The hard work of such a large orchard had been good for his physique. His hair had darkened some underneath, but blonde strands endured on the outermost layer, evidence of his long days spent under the hot sun. It framed his face and fell to his jaw in jagged ends.

While Katiyana and Jeremy grew in beauty and young life, Barney deteriorated. He yielded to despair time and time again; he constantly asked Jeremy to replace his bottle of ale, and slowly, gradually, he became unrecognizable. He would yell at Katiyana for something as small as not having his meal ready exactly when he wanted it, and then, once Katiyana went back outside, he agonized over how poorly he'd treated her. He'd rock in his chair, crying, mumbling apologies to his dead nephew. And then he'd pick up his bottle and drink some more. To his credit, yelling was the worst Barney did. But seeing how often he drank, watching the degenerating effect it had, I feared more would come of it.

One day, Jeremy arrived as usual, smiling huge at seeing Katiyana. They'd become quite fond of each other over the years.

"What's that?" Katiyana asked when she saw him, returning the smile. She stopped pumping water long enough to get a look at the basket he carried.

"I made us a picnic," he said.

When Jeremy got close enough, Katiyana reached her hand into the bucket of water and splashed some in his face. "What for?"

He splashed her back. "Does there need to be a reason?" He opened the basket for her to look.

"Jam?" she asked in astonishment. "And honey? Where did you get all of this?"

"From the market yesterday."

A look of fear formed on Katiyana's face. "You didn't use Barney's money, did you?"

Jeremy spoke softly. "Of course not. I'd never do that."

Katiyana looked embarrassed for a moment before lifting the bucket of water and taking it into the barn for the goats.

"I wish you would have come with me yesterday."

Katiyana moved with purpose now, forking a measure of hay to give to the horse.

Jeremy took it from her. "Let me help."

Katiyana watched him. "I've told you. He won't let me go to the market."

Jeremy threw the hay into the horse's stall, then rested the pitchfork on the ground, leaning on it and looking at his friend. "How would he even know?

You could just let him think you were out on one of your walks across the orchard."

"I couldn't deceive him." She shook her head. "Really, Jeremy, I wish you'd stop asking."

"All right," he said. "I won't ask you anymore, but if you ever change your mind, the offer is always good." He set the pitchfork down and grabbed the picnic basket again. "I brought something for you." He reached into the basket and pulled out a book with a brightly colored picture on the front

He held it out to her and she took it, running her fingertips across the cover.

"It's a different kind of paper than they use for books now." He opened it to show her. "And the binding's old." Jeremy tipped the book so she could see how the pages were glued to the cover.

"Did you get it at the market?" she asked solemnly.

"No, it's something I've had for a while. I thought you would like it. I've read it enough to have it memorized."

"Thank you," she said, her eyes still focused on the image of the cover—sheep dotting a valley surrounded by rocky hills and lush green landscape. "It's beautiful."

"You're welcome. We can start reading it on our picnic. I brought some bread too—"

"Oh, I almost forgot!" she blurted out. She turned and ran into the house. A wall of harsh words waited for her.

"What have you done?" Barney yelled just after she entered. "It smells horrible in here!"

"Sorry, Uncle Barney." Katiyana grabbed the paddle and reached into the oven for a blackened loaf of bread.

"You never do anything right! Jeremy could run this kitchen better than you!" He looked disgraceful with his shirt buttoned wrong and his hair a mess. His belly had grown significantly over the years and protruded far over his belt

Jeremy came in through the kitchen door, watching warily.

"Please don't yell at me, Uncle Barney. It was an accident."

"And you left the kitchen window open all night! It's freezing in here!" He stumbled closer to Katiyana. She cringed at his oncoming rage. I cringed as well, hating that someone so low dared to yell at the princess.

"Sir, don't—" Jeremy began.

"Shut up, Jeremy Simkins! Keep your nose out of where it doesn't belong!" He turned back to Katiyana. "You are worse than a Simkins! I hate that you ever came here!"

"Well, maybe I hate that I ever came here too," Katiyana shot back. Rarely did she talk back to him, and never during an outburst. I was surprised, but perhaps she'd simply grown tired of it or realized that protecting herself was more important than respecting what Barney had become.

Without warning, Barney swung his fist in Katiyana's direction, hitting her in the neck.

Jeremy acted immediately. He shoved Barney away from Katiyana, sending him backward against the kitchen wall. Then Jeremy reached for the princess. "Are you all right?"

She held her neck, her eyes wide, as if she felt more shock than pain.

It horrified me to watch it all. I wondered if the spell I'd muttered when she first came to Barney had ever taken life. Would the winter wind protect her? If so, where was that protection now?

Jeremy faced Barney. "How dare you hit her," he fumed.

"Shut up, Jeremy Simkins. The girl is no business of yours."

"Jeremy, please stop. Let's go back outside," Katiyana pleaded.

"No," Jeremy said. "I'm not going to let him get away with what he did."

"What are you going to do about it? And why do you care anyway?" Then it looked as if something dawned on Barney. "Wait a minute. You two haven't been courting or anything, have you?"

"No, Uncle," Katiyana answered emphatically.

"No, sir," Jeremy said, but he stood down a bit

after that. He crossed his arms and lowered his head.

"You're fired, Jeremy Simkins. Don't come back, and don't ever come near the girl again."

Jeremy looked back up at his employer. "But it's right in the middle of harvest."

"The girl's seventeen now. She can manage everything on her own. We don't need you anymore."

"But, Uncle, you won't even let me go to the market," Katiyana protested

"The horse can lead me well enough," Barney said. He let out a burp, making him look more ridiculous and less credible than ever. "I'm sure the horse is smarter than a Simkins anyway."

"But, sir," Jeremy began.

"Get out!" Barney sneered.

Jeremy looked at Katiyana. Neither one of them seemed to know what to say or do. So Jeremy left.

Barney turned away from the princess and felt his way along the wall back to the rocking chair, slanted and stumbling the whole time. Katiyana watched him. Then she took the book Jeremy had given her up to her room and placed it under her pillow.

Katiyana finished the day's work alone, collecting barrel after barrel of apples and loading them into the cart. But without Jeremy, it would be at least another day before the cart filled, and Barney took that delay out on the princess of Mayhem with spiteful words and an angry fist.

Farewell

Nothing could have prepared me for this misfortune that befell our lovely princess. Not only had fate deprived her of a loving mother and father, but now her only family betrayed her, and her only friend had walked away.

To my surprise, however, Jeremy returned the next day. Relief swelled in my breast at seeing him, thinking he would cheer the princess. But there was also apprehension, since Barney had so clearly expressed his wishes that Jeremy stay away. Early in the morning, Katiyana saw him coming through the orchard toward the barn. She ducked inside and began giving the animals their breakfast.

Jeremy appeared at the doorway just after she had thrown hay into the horse's stall. He watched her carefully, his eyes following her every delicate move.

"Are you all right?" he asked.

Katiyana dug the metal scoop into the chicken feed again and again, giving the chickens more to peck at than they could eat in a chicken's lifetime.

Jeremy reached out for her hand. "Come on, Kat. What are you doing? Barney will be furious if the feed is wasted."

But the princess of Mayhem continued on, throwing chicken feed all over the ground. The boy grabbed hold of her chin and forced her to look at him. Only then did he see what I had been exposed to the night before: her perfect face covered in splotchy black and blue.

"What happened?"

Silence.

"Kat, why didn't you hide from him? It's not like he can see you."

"That's easy for you to say, isn't it?" She returned to the chicken feed, this time scraping the excess off the ground and putting it back in the feed sack.

"Help me understand then. Why didn't you hide from him?" Jeremy bent down and helped the princess clear the feed. Greedy chickens tried to peck them away.

"It just took me by surprise," she defended. "I had no time to even consider what to do." She shook her head and dumped the last scoop of feed back into the sack. "He's all I have."

"I came back to see if he had cooled off and changed his mind, but from the looks of it . . ." He nodded toward Katiyana's face. Jeremy hung his head for a moment. "Kat, I don't know what to do."

"What do you mean? Shouldn't you find another job? Barney's not going to let you in the house again. It doesn't seem that complicated to me."

In earnest he grabbed hold of one of her arms. "He doesn't have to know. I'll come during the day and help you work. He can take the apples to market if he wants, but he doesn't have to know I'm even here. I can't lose this job, Kat. I can't lose—"

Katiyana studied his eager eyes. "He's blind, Jeremy. He's not stupid. Besides, how will you earn money for your family if you work here without pay? I certainly couldn't pay you. What about your younger brothers and sisters?"

Jeremy pulled his arms away from her. "So you want me to go?"

Katiyana gave a nod, her face tight.

Jeremy stared at her for several more seconds, twisting the rim of his worn hat in his hands and thinking, as if formulating a plan. Then he walked out of the barn.

Once alone, Katiyana let out a long breath, sending a small white cloud of warmth into the cold air before heading back to the house.

Barney greeted her at the door and wasted no

time ordering the poor girl around. "Get to work. There will be no rest for you now, doing double. I hope you're satisfied. You and your lover."

Katiyana glared at him.

How tragic! Barney had held onto specks of decency for all those years. Always before, he had apologized after yelling at her, occasionally expressed his love, and even let out a sincere compliment from time to time. But the ale got the better of him, so now only the worst remained.

"He's not my lover," she said coldly. "And he's not coming back."

"Well, I'm glad to hear it." He turned away and sat at the table. "Cook me some eggs."

She glared a little longer, but eventually succumbed to his order, cracking two eggs and opening them over a pot of simmering water.

Such tense emotions filled that little house all day. Katiyana scowled as she scrubbed more vigorously than usual, swept more forcefully, and occasionally let go of a silent, streaky tear. Every time Barney came into a room, Katiyana quickly left, unless he required her to make a meal, start a fire, or go over the record books with him. What pain it caused me to watch her, what sorrow. I felt such a responsibility for her, being the only person besides Barney that knew of her circumstances and station in life. And yet, I could do nothing. Nothing. An intense knot formed in my stomach that day as I worried about her. What would come of her now? What could she possibly do?

When Katiyana finished her work that day and Barney lay snoozing on his bed—meaning the apples would wait still another day to go to the market—the princess sneaked out to watch the sunset. Creeping away from the house, she crossed the portion of the orchard that led to a bluff. Rocks jutted out, forming a natural staircase. She climbed to the top and sat on a patch of dried grass, wrapping her tattered shawl tightly around her shoulders. Bubbling storm clouds sped in, creating a masterpiece of pinks, oranges, and blues, the only color she had access to in her bleak world. The colors soon faded, giving way to the gray of a tempest and the shivery damp of rain. Yet she remained, seemingly unaware of everything but the thoughts in her head. What could she have been thinking? In that moment I wished the mirror's powers extended to mind reading. Would she leave her home? Where would she go? Would she stay and face the possibility of more abuse? I couldn't bear it! My heartbeat quickened as I frantically worried over the girl, and hated that I could do nothing to help her.

Suddenly, as if coming out of a trance, Katiyana became aware of the raindrops pouncing on her and the ground all around her. She stood and began to make her way back down the bluff, but in the swelling darkness she struggled to keep her balance on the path. In a matter of moments, the wind intensified and the rain turned to hail. Katiyana pulled her shawl up and wrapped it around her head for cover. Just as she reached the bottom of the bluff, she rounded a tree—and ran straight into Jeremy Simkins.

Katiyana fell back in surprise, grasping at the gnarled shrubbery to keep from tumbling to the ground. She did not look happy to see him. "Jeremy Simkins, what are you doing here?" The tree jutted out from the rocks and formed a rainbow over their heads, giving them some shelter from the rain.

He watched her shocked, rain-streaked face for a moment. "Kat, I . . . I don't know how to say this."

"Then don't. Jeremy, you can't keep coming around—"

"I love you," he blurted.

Katiyana stopped. Her lips froze; her eyes froze; I wondered if her heart stopped beating.

"I love you," Jeremy repeated softly.

I did not envy Jeremy in that moment: handing Katiyana his heart on a platter when she didn't seem interested.

"You love me?" she finally asked. "How can you love me?"

His smitten smile could have answered for him, but he spoke just the same. "How can I not?"

Now, I usually didn't keep track of time. There was really no point given where I was. But that moment seemed to stretch on for hours, neither breathing a single word, getting soaked to the bone in all that rain.

Finally, Jeremy spoke again. "Kat, I'm sure this isn't going to make any sense, but . . ." He reached out for her stiff, wet hands, looking at them affectionately. "I have to leave. There are some things I need to take care of."

"What things?" Confusion appeared in her blue eyes, asking for an explanation. She tilted her head in an attempt to get him to look at her, but he would not.

Jeremy looked her in the eye, his brow determined. "I can't tell you everything right now. I have to find a way to earn more money soon or I'll be—" He stumbled for words, looking away from her again. What on earth was Jeremy Simkins hiding? "It could be dangerous for me." He met her gaze once more. "But I can't leave you here with your uncle, either. You are too important to me. I have to know that you are safe from him."

"I can't go with you! I can't leave him!" Katiyana said in a panic, shaking her head and trying to pull her hands away from him.

Jeremy tightened his grip, holding fast to her long fingers as he continued to gaze into her worried eyes. He spoke soothingly, except for a tiny fraction of insistence. "No, you can't go with me. That's not what I meant." He closed his eyes as if searching for the right words. "I know this must be so hard to understand." Opening his eyes once more, he spoke with the greatest intensity I'd ever heard from him. "But, Kat, you must leave your uncle."

"You expect me just to give up everything because you say so?"

Jeremy released her hands and threw his arms up in exasperation. "Give up everything? Kat, what do you have here?" He ran his fingers through his hair as he spun around full circle, a look of frustration on his face, and then paused, taking a moment to fill his lungs with fresh air. He took several breaths and placed his hands on his hips, proceeding with new-found composure. "Kat, there is so much more to life than what you have here. I can show you that."

Katiyana bowed her head. "I can't. He won't tell me why, but he says I'm never to leave the orchard."

Jeremy leaned toward her and argued his point with zeal. "He won't let you because he wants to control you. He doesn't want to share you. Can't you see that? As long as you stay here, he'll have his food cooked and his apples picked."

Katiyana spoke with equal enthusiasm, leaning further toward her friend. "It's more than that—it has to be. He won't even let me go to the market, and he never has, even before he went blind and started drinking. He says it's dangerous."

Jeremy nodded, again finding his naturally unruf-
fled temperament. "I've been to the market," he said.
"Sure, there's danger, but I've never seen anyone with
the bruises you've got on your face."

Self-conscious, Katiyana put a hand to her purple
cheek.

"It's dangerous here. Barney doesn't want what's
best for you."

"And you do?" she asked.

Jeremy answered in perfect mildness. "Yes." The
tenderness in his eyes touched me. What gratitude
filled my heart in that moment, for I'd never seen
a truer friend. "I have something for you." Jeremy
reached inside the sack strapped around his shoulder.
"I wish I had more," he said, holding out a package
wrapped in butcher paper.

Katiyana's look softened as she reached forward
and gently rested her fingers on the package before
pulling it toward her. "A present?" Katiyana stared
at it with wistful eyes. She studied the neat wrappings and shoestring ribbon as she cradled the cherished bundle. "I haven't had a present since I was a
little girl. Barney used to give one to me every year
on the same day. He called it my birthday but said
he didn't know what my real birthday was." Tears
welled up in her eyes, slow and steady, the way a pail
of fresh cow milk fills to the top. Perhaps, like me,
she remembered how he had once been. Memories of

him, good ones, swarmed in my mind like the distant buzz of noise when you are mostly asleep. And it hurt me to watch her, to see her pain. "He used to call me his little kitten. I don't know what happened, why he stopped loving me." She looked to Jeremy. "I don't know if I can leave him."

Jeremy readjusted the sack hanging from his shoulder. "Open it."

Katiyana pulled at one end of the shoestring and tore the paper away, revealing a wooden box carved with clouds and stars. Carefully, shielding the box with her body from the rain trickling through the branches above them, she lifted off the lid. A heavy pouch lay inside.

"It's my earnings, minus what I had to give to my family. There's six years worth. It's yours now."

"I don't understand." She shook her head.

"I don't want you to go back to your uncle. I love you. And I want to take care of you."

"Jeremy, what are you talking about? I know we've been friends, good friends even, but I don't . . ."

"I want to marry you."

That seemed to get the princess's attention more than anything else he'd said so far. "When?" she inquired, a look of disbelief spreading across her face.

"I told you I have some things to take care of first. Kat, I want you to take this money—it is enough to live on for at least a year."

"But you won't be gone that long, will you?" For the first time the confusion in her eyes dissipated, replaced entirely by fear. Wide-eyed, she waited breathlessly for reassurance.

"I hope not." He closed the remaining distance between them and rested his forehead on hers. "I don't know how long I can stand being away from you. But the things I have to take care of are absolutely necessary if we are to be together." And he meant it, judging by the sincerity in his voice, the honesty in his brow, the longing in his eyes.

This calmed Katiyana slightly, but she continued to voice her doubts. "I still don't know if I can leave him. Where am I to go?"

Jeremy was the only other person she had ever known, aside from Barney. Would she really be able to leave her uncle? How could she survive on her own? Without a roof over her head? Without food to eat? Without Jeremy? But she had the money, and apparently, an offer of marriage. I liked Jeremy well enough, but marry the princess? Then again, I reasoned, perhaps it really would be better for her to live a common life. After all, what were the alternatives? Be discovered by the queen and face an early death? All things considered, I made an effort to swallow my initial disapproval.

"You don't have to decide now. When I am ready, I will find you, no matter how long I have to look."

Jeremy pulled back, peering deep into Katiyana's eyes and caressing her face with his fingertips. The rain had finally stopped, though the clouds continued to thicken and blacken. "When you leave, if you leave, there is a man named Juno at the market. He works at the platform on the north end where they sell unclaimed property and things like that. He is a friend of mine. Tell him that you know me and he will help you find lodging. He can be trusted."

"But . . ."

"Use the money with care. Don't let anyone know you have it."

"But . . ."

"I'm sorry that I don't have more to give you. And I'm sorry that I have to leave you now." He leaned forward, glancing at her lips, his hand still gently stroking her face. "Kat Whyte," he spoke softly.

"But . . ."

Jeremy covered her lips with his, giving one last manifestation of his previous confessions. Katiyana didn't even have the chance to respond to his kiss. "Good-bye," he whispered, before turning away from her and bolting into a run. The determination on his face masked any regret, and his sodden feet sent off splashes of muddy water with every pounding step.

"Wait!" she called, running after him through the foggy dim. "Wait!" She followed him all the way to the house, but his figure melted in the distance.

Out of breath, Katiyana stumbled to her knees, eyes straining to see the last glimpse of her friend until he vanished altogether.

Katiyana knelt there long after he'd gone, drenched, her face a mixture of sadness and confusion. The goats cried in the background, their noisy demands for feed finally pulling the princess out of her stupor. Slowly, she rose to her feet, slogging into the dark barn to feed the animals. Inside, Katiyana stowed the box Jeremy had given her beneath some hay. She stayed in the barn for hours, fiddling with straw and smudging her face with dirt as she wiped away tears.

I couldn't explain Jeremy's mysteriousness, and his secrecy made me nervous, pulling his character under scrutiny. Most of the time, I used the powers of the mirror to focus solely on the princess of Mayhem. I knew then that I should have kept a closer eye on the boy she spent every passing day with. I had followed him home once, but a single night of peeking in on the Simkins' was more than enough for me—thirteen children! What a mess of people and things and noise! What could Jeremy possibly have to take care of unless it involved his horrible, rambunctious family? Was it enough to justify encouraging the princess to go off on her own? I vowed to watch him with greater interest, despite the unpleasantness of his home.

Katiyana eventually went into the house. She lit a candle in the kitchen, illuminating her unusually pale, clammy skin and black hair—the wet, clumpy strands stuck to her head, face, shoulders, and upper back. Barney still snoozed. She watched him, perhaps waiting to see if he'd wake. I longed to know her thoughts, the feelings of her heart, but her emotions hid behind a face of stone.

Katiyana stepped up the rickety staircase and prepared for bed—slipping into her white, ruffled nightgown and hanging her dress and shawl on separate hooks near the window. She crept back down the stairs and took a seat in front of the ever dwindling, smoky fire. While in an uninterrupted daydream, she alternately brushed her hair and rubbed it between her hands until dry. Whether or not she reached a decision that night, I cannot say. After dousing the fire, she climbed the stairs, crawled under her bed covers, and gave into exhaustion.

❧ ✳ ☙

In the morning, Barney commanded her to make him breakfast. She refused. When he threatened to hurt her, she stood firm. When he tried to swing, she ducked. Around the room they went, Katiyana hiding, and Barney stumbling after her. Finally he grabbed hold of her arm and hit the side of her face, sending her to the floor. She scurried away from him and, struggling to hold back tears, Katiyana moved toward the door. "Good-bye, Uncle," she murmured just before walking out.

He went after her, stumbling toward the door, but did not brave the porch steps. "Kat!" he called. "Come back here!"

Katiyana went to the barn and fed the animals one last time. Such a thoughtful girl! She retrieved Jeremy's gift of money and packed a sack of apples before starting out, trekking across the orchard and out onto the road that led to Mischief. I knew it hurt her to walk away, because even when Barney's house couldn't be seen anymore, she continued to look back.

To Market

I watched earnestly as Princess Katiyana made her way down the road to Mischief. What would become of her? Maybe she hadn't been taught as much as she should have been, but she knew how to reason, and was willing to learn. I predicted she would do well on her own, have a few adventures and invaluable experiences. But at the same time, I worried for her. Greatly.

The brightness that morning deceived me; I longed to be in the sunshine. But Katiyana pulled her shawl close and tight, and in no time began to shiver.

The road to Mischief ran straight, other than a few gentle curves, and no other roads connected to it between Barney's orchard and the market, so the princess found her way with ease. She made the long walk in good time, arriving before sunset, having munched on the apples she'd brought. The market came into her view, and knowing her history, it's no surprise she slowed her pace, savoring each sight, sound, and smell. With wide eyes, she watched men and boys walk about on tall sticks for the entertainment of shoppers; women carried babes and baskets and bushels of barley; a young girl held out a container of grapes, hoping to make a sale; children ran about in boisterous laughter, chasing and stopping and catching. Eventually, her expressions of wonder turned to a joyful but timid smile.

Watching the princess take in the wonders of Mischief Market for the first time proved to be superior entertainment. Her bright eyes flitted from one spectacle to another as she weaved through passes lined with large, canvas tents and worn, wooden stands on wheels. It tortured me to see her smelling sage and autumn lilies and tasting cinnamon roasted almonds; how I hated that the powers of the mirror limited me to sight and sound alone.

The final pass forced the princess to turn right, and nothing captured her attention like the male dwarf standing on a platform in the distance. She approached with delicate, cautious steps, a look of curiosity radiating from her eyes.

"Who will have him?" a voice yelled.

The princess studied the man who had spoken, a

beast of a fellow with a beard and a belly and unkempt clothing. He strode across the platform, gesturing with a coiled whip at the diminutive figure stooped in the center. As Katiyana looked on in dismay, he yanked back the small man's head with a sharp tug at his black hair.

"Who will have him?" the beastly man repeated.

The crowd gathered in front of the platform shifted and murmured until a single hand rose above their heads. "Aye! I'll take him . . . if you give me a gold coin."

The group roared in laughter.

"Nay, but I'll only ask a pair of silver coins."

Tearing her eyes away, Katiyana tapped the shoulder of a man near the back of the group. "Excuse me, sir. Is this the north platform?"

He turned and gave her a considering look. "Why, yes," he answered kindly. A sudden whip crack startled them both, drawing their eyes back to the platform and the short figure cowering under the lash. Katiyana and the man next to her both winced, as did many, but others cheered, shouting and raising celebratory fists in the air. The man inflicting pain shoved the small man—who scooted a few steps but otherwise remained steady—and spat on the top of his head.

As if she couldn't stand watching further, Katiyana abruptly asked another question. "Excuse me," Katiyana said again. "Do you know where I can find a man named Juno?"

"That's him up there," he answered, pointing to the whipping man.

This caused me to wonder again at Jeremy's character—sending the princess to get help from a man even more abusive that the one she just left.

Katiyana slipped a hand inside her bag of apples, where Jeremy's box of money also rested. She had never even opened the pouch. Were the coins she possessed gold or silver? Her hand moved through the pile of apples until it brushed across the box. She struggled to get the lid off with one hand. Finally, she loosened the tie around the pouch and pulled a few coins up and out of the bag. Silver.

The large, bearded man began making a joke of the miniature man. "He cooks," he said as he placed a bonnet on his head. "He cleans." Now an apron was placed around his neck, and after that a broom shoved in his hand. "He even knows how to tend to the little ones." Juno reached down and pulled a baby from his mother's arms and handed it to the little man, who looked severely displeased. I can't say I blamed him.

A few members of the crowd doubled over in laughter, heaving and wheezing. "What will you give for such a worthy slave? I ask only two silver coins." He held up two large, chubby fingers to the crowd. The baby began to cry and was handed back down to his mother.

I admit, I was so enthralled with the scene that it

surprised me when Katiyana spoke up. "I will take him." Her voice faltered amid the shouting and hilarity of the crowd. With gritted, dirty teeth, Juno threw his whip into the back of the little man, causing him to fall to his child-sized knees.

"I will take him!" Katiyana yelled. A few of the people quieted and looked around, trying to see where the voice had come from. She jerked an apple from her bag and launched it toward the platform. It flew through the air until it hit the front edge of the stage and split, sending apple shards in all directions.

"I will take him!"

Her final shout was followed by an eerie silence. Her feet remained firmly grounded as she stood tall, focusing all her attention on the men atop the platform rather than the dozens of eyes staring at her.

"Well, come and get him, then." Juno motioned her forward.

Katiyana moved steadily through the crowd, stopping just in front of the little man on the platform. Juno bent down toward her to finalize the deal. Without looking at him, the princess dropped the coins into his outstretched, oversized hands.

"Stupid girl," he muttered after inspecting her payment. "I only asked for two silver coins and she's given me two whole doces." He laughed as he grabbed the small man by the shirt and thrust him off the platform.

"Juno, is it?" Kat asked forcefully as the large, cruel man shuffled away.

He turned toward her once more. "Who cares to know?" he shot back.

Katiyana's eyes narrowed. She lifted her chin and turned away, giving no more attention to Jeremy's supposed friend.

Noticing her newly acquired charge, she helped the little man to his feet and dusted him off, her efforts frustrated by his frantic attempts to rip off the bonnet and apron. His head, covered in bushy, dark hair, stood just a few short inches above her navel, and I wondered if his black eyes ever looked anything but annoyed. His ears, nose, and mouth all looked too big for his face, but his eyes fit just right.

"Now what?" the princess asked her new slave.

"You tell me! You're the one who bought me. What, you want me to think of work to do for you?" The man threw his stubby arms up in exasperation. "I never heard of a slave who had to think for his master."

"I don't have any work for you to do." Katiyana smiled down at him. "Oh," she reconsidered. "You can carry my pack if you'd like."

"No, I wouldn't like," he said.

"Oh."

His tone displeased me. Katiyana had only acted out of pity, attempting to free him from humiliation. Now it appeared the little man wanted to humiliate her.

"Well, where do you live? It's late."

He was right; the sun was setting. But what could she tell him now?

"I don't live anywhere." Such an honest girl!

"You mean you don't have any place to live? Why are you taking on a slave if you don't have any place to live?"

"I never meant to take on a slave, I just . . ."

"Never mind," he huffed. "Follow me."

The crowd dispersed rapidly once the auction was over, the last few stragglers making their final selections for the day as the shop owners began to close down. The sun disappeared behind the tall, surrounding trees of the forest, casting long, leafy shadows at the princess's feet. Katiyana paused to watch, enjoying each moment of her newfound freedom.

The tiny man had gone off during her reverie, and despite his short stature he moved quite fast. Katiyana had to run to catch up to him as he headed away from the market and out of town. She followed him, I imagine, because she didn't know what else to do.

All the noise of the market dimmed to nothing as they walked into Fluttering Forest. Katiyana struggled to keep up, peering all around her as if she expected something to jump out and eat her. The waking hoot of an owl sounded above, forcing her eyes upward to see. She slowed and turned about, looking in all directions until the sound of little legs bustling through fallen autumn leaves grew too distant. Katiyana hurried to catch up, and once she did, the glow of a small house came into view.

The little man turned around. "Maybe you don't have a place to live. But I do." He motioned his thumb toward his chest.

"Where should I stay then?"

The little man debated. I hoped he would do something to help the princess. She had bought him after all, and by law had claim over him. But perhaps by now he could tell that she didn't realize it. Was he considering escape? And if so, why had he led her to his home?

A muffled voice sounded from inside the house. "I'm going out for a pee."

"Keeping a lady around would not be such a good idea," the small man muttered. "Hide," he whispered loudly.

"Why should we hide?"

But he had already clasped his pudgy fingers around her arm and begun pulling her behind a tree. "Close your eyes," he said as they ducked. He peeked around to see the back of his fellow dwarf. Katiyana obeyed. "And your ears."

"What's going on?" she asked. "I can't close my ears anyway."

The little man mumbled something to himself,

waiting as his acquaintance unbuttoned his trousers around the corner of the house.

"Are you going to tell me what's going on?" Katiyana repeated.

The other little man heard the chatter and quickly finished his business. He turned and looked about with suspicious eyes. "Who's there?" he called.

Neither Katiyana nor her little slave responded as the other man closed the short distance between them.

"What are we hiding for?"

Agitated, the dwarf answered. "Because I haven't decided what to do with you yet!"

"Kurz, is that you?"

Katiyana peeked out from behind the tree. She stared in amazement upon discovering there was not just one little man, but two.

"Stay here," her bondsman insisted. Then he took a deep breath and stepped out from behind the tree.

The eyes of the other little man widened. "It is you! Kurz, you've escaped, you devil." Then he began calling to the others still in the house. What peculiar names they had—Corto and Jab (or something like that) and a few more. "Kurz is back! Come and see."

One by one they paraded out. Seven in all, including Kurz. And what a sight, congratulating and hugging with the shortest arms I'd ever seen in or out of the mirror.

Kurz told his story of being captured, humiliated, and sold to the most peculiar master.

"You haven't brought him here, have you? He'll enslave us all!" one of them shouted in fear.

"It's not a him," Kurz corrected. "And I'm pretty sure she doesn't want any of us for a slave." He looked back to the tree where Katiyana hid from the others. "You can come out now."

"He has brought his master!" Oh, the commotion that followed, six little men trying at the same time to get back into the tiny door of the cozy-looking house. Katiyana stepped out from behind the tree and watched the frenzy in bewilderment. After the last dwarf had made it through the door, it closed and locked with a loud click.

"What do we do now?" Katiyana asked.

"What do you mean we?" Kurz grumbled, heading toward the house.

"You would just leave me out here?" Katiyana had an astonished look on her face. She looked about the surrounding forest. Full night had set in, and chill wind had picked up. I could only imagine her thoughts.

Kurz paused, still facing the house and away from Katiyana. I could see the dilemma clearly in his eyes.

He looked back at her. "This is no place for a girl."

It wasn't a no, but it wasn't a yes either.

"Kurz?" she pleaded.

He groaned loudly and finally motioned for her to follow him. He muttered a slew of words as he led the princess to the house. I couldn't quite distinguish what he said, but I'm pretty sure he wasn't exactly thrilled to be letting her into his home.

And the other dwarves wouldn't allow it; they kept the door securely locked as the princess and her little man approached. Kurz knocked. "Open up, you imbeciles!"

No answer.

"So where did you come from?" Kurz asked, knocking again.

Of course, she couldn't tell. She shook her head.

"Okay, where is it you're going?"

That question she could answer. "I don't have anyplace to go."

"Then what is it you're supposed to be doing?"

"I'm waiting."

"What are you waiting for?"

"I'm not sure."

"All right then, who are you waiting for?"

"Jeremy Simkins."

"Really?" he asked.

Katiyana nodded.

"Now, you don't want to be dealing with anyone by the name of Simkins. Every one of them's been nothing but trouble since anyone can remember. If you've met any Simkins, every dwarf in the kingdom of Mischief will have pity on you.

He knocked again, this time a bit more forcefully.

"How many dwarves are there in Mischief?"

"Seven."

Seven Tiny Men

"Open this door!" Kurz yelled. "She's been wronged by a Simkins."

"No, no, he hasn't wronged me," Katiyana tried to defend.

"Just knowing one is being wronged."

The door finally opened. Such a sight, seven little men! Upon closer inspection, it was more like five and two halves, for two of the men were stuck together. A stranger thing I'm sure I've never seen, and I couldn't help but be distracted wondering how they functioned.

Every possession fit neatly in the home's only room. A brick oven and a workspace for food preparation took up the right side of the room; a round table circled with stools stood right before the entrance;

and a brick fireplace barely burned to Katiyana's left, surrounded by a disarray of blankets, pillows, and dwarf-sized stools. Kurz motioned to one such stool, inviting the princess to take a seat.

Katiyana sat, enthralled as Kurz introduced each of the others.

"This is Jalb," he said, poking a stocky finger at a stocky bald man that with greater height could have passed for a sea pirate. "He's the domestic one. All that shoving a bonnet on my head and an apron around my neck! This is the one who wears the apron around here. And he actually likes it."

Jalb stood up from his wide, sturdy stool and took a begrudging bow. "Can I finish making dinner now? I'm starving."

"Make enough for the girl. She'll be staying for dinner." Kurz's request was met with a grunt, but since Jalb obeyed, I couldn't help suspect that the dwarf valued Kurz's opinion. In fact, Kurz's confident air and the way in which the other dwarves surrounded and listened to him intently made me think he was the most respected.

The two dwarves connected together got introduced next. "This is Corto," Kurz said as he placed a hand on the shoulder of the man on the left. Only their middles merged together; each man had all the normal appendages. Kurz moved to the other side of the men. "And this is Arrapato." Arrapato, who looked identical to his brother, gave a nod. Both the men had wide, open eyes the color of coal and were thinner than most of the others. One wore his dark hair slightly longer than the other. I couldn't then imagine how they managed to find clothing. Perhaps they simply dressed as normal men and cut a hole in the side of their shirts and pants to accommodate their brother. "These two earn most of our bread. You'd be amazed what people pay just to get a look at them."

Kurz's attention moved to two more dwarves sitting on low stools. "This here is Duan," he said with his finger in the face of the pudgiest of them all. "He and Kapos here do the gardening. A man's got to eat, you know." Duan looked to be the oldest and was mostly bald except for some wisps of white hair near the back of his head. Kapos was much younger and had a pleasant face. I imagine he could have been a lady's man if his stature had not been so small. He nodded and winked at Katiyana as a bit of his long, straight hair fell from behind his ear and swept across his forehead.

What a pleasure it was to see her then, smiling at them all, truly enjoying herself for the first time in days. But an uncertainty lingered in my heart and mind. I thought of Jeremy and the words Kurz had said about the Simkins family. I worried for the princess, and made up my mind that as soon as she settled in, I would locate Jeremy Simkins and see what he was up to. Would the dwarves, as Kurz had implied, have pity on her and give her shelter?

One more dwarf remained. "This is Pokole," Kurz said. "And he's the man of the house." All of the dwarves nodded and grunted in agreement. I wondered how old he could be—he still looked so much like a child. He had pale yellow hair and light blue eyes. Pokole also sat on a stool, but his legs hung off the end, several inches from the floor. When standing, he probably would have come to just above Katiyana's knee, and a normal man could have wrapped his hands around the tiny man's waist. His arms twisted a bit as well, giving me the impression that he was frail and slightly deformed. "Be careful with Pokole, though. He breaks easy."

"What do you mean he breaks easy?" Katiyana asked, speaking for the first time.

"His bones," Kapos explained, unable to keep from smiling at the pretty lady in his house. "His bones break easy. Sometimes he'll crack if you do nothing but give him a slap on the back."

"Doesn't he speak?" Katiyana asked.

"He's a little shy around strangers," Kapos answered.

"Just don't touch him," Kurz broke in protectively. "He does what he can to help us all."

Jalb took one last testing sip of his stew.

"Dinner's on! Enough of all this girly chitchat."

"Wait," said Kurz. "We haven't heard the girl's story."

"Yeah, we don't even know her name," said

Kapos, sending a flirtatious smile Katiyana's way.

"But can't it wait?" whined Jalb. "I'm starving."

"Oh, the stew will keep, you wretch. Let's hear the girl." Kurz's dominance showed once again. I don't think any of them dared to argue with him.

"Yeah, I want to hear about the girl," Corto said. Arrapato nodded in agreement.

I felt nervous for her—her first real test. I wondered if she would be true to Barney's commands and avoid telling her real name or where she came from.

"Oh, you don't want to hear about me," she said, trying to brush it off.

"Okay, let's eat," Jalb said.

"Shhhhh," Kurz commanded. "Yes, we do want to hear about you. And about that Simkins too."

Katiyana thought and thought while six pair of eyes stared in anticipation. Jalb played with a pile of potato peels, looking terribly put out. I noticed for the first time that he had to stand on top of a stool to reach the work area in the kitchen.

What could she tell these seven little men? I imagine she wondered why Barney had never let her leave the orchard and if it really could be dangerous to reveal where she came from. But I sensed the dwarves were trustworthy; I hoped she would confide in them.

"I was raised by my uncle Barney on an apple orchard."

"Wait, give us your name first," Duan interrupted.

All the dwarves leaned in, eager to hear the name of the pretty maiden in front of them.

"Kat."

Each dwarf face pulled a look of shock or wonder or disgrace. "Your name is Cat?" Kurz asked. "As in the animal?"

"No," Katiyana said. "It's spelled K-A-T, not C-A-T."

"Oh, I see," voiced several of the dwarves, nodding and shifting in their seats. I guessed most of them didn't know how to spell anything.

"Oh, it must be short for something," Corto guessed.

"Yeah," Arrapato agreed. "Maybe her real name is Katarina or Katcha or Katalyn."

At this point I smiled, knowing the dwarves were on to something. But even Katiyana did not know her full name.

"No," Katiyana said. "It's just Kat." She looked around at them all as a bit of red seeped into her otherwise tan face. "Kat Whyte."

"Well, what else can you tell us?" Kurz inquired further.

"I love books and reading and drawing."

"What else?" Kapos chimed.

"What about your family?" Duan asked. "Where are your mother and father?"

"I really don't know anything else. Living on an apple orchard and my uncle Barney are all I know."

"What about that Simkins? Was he the one who left your face looking so awful?" Jalb questioned, suspicion evident in his eyes and the way he crossed his arms over his chest. Despite his rough edges, he actually seemed to care about the girl, at least where Jeremy Simkins played a part.

Katiyana's face really did look awful. The bruises were dark and stood out in sharp contrast with her skin.

Katiyana looked at the floor, the fire casting light on her dark hair and still face. "No, no, it was nothing like that. Jeremy worked at the orchard. I don't know much about him either, except that he always kept me company. I thought we were just good friends. Then one day he told me he loved me."

"Loved you and then left you," Kurz said, voicing his disapproval.

"How did you end up here?" Duan wondered aloud.

"Jeremy told me to leave my uncle."

"Now, why would he do a thing like that?" Jalb asked, pounding a fist into the palm of his opposite hand.

"He thought my uncle was dangerous."

"And was he?" Duan sought.

Katiyana hesitated, touching her bruised face lightly, but perhaps remembering the good things her uncle had done for her. "At times," she admitted with a regretful nod.

A profound hush fell over them all. Their confused faces were readable enough: if Jeremy Simkins was so rotten, why help the girl and try to protect her from Barney?

"Well, any fool can fall in love," Kurz remarked.

"Maybe it's got nothing to do with love," Jalb offered. "He is a Simkins, after all, and they're known liars and thieves. Maybe telling you he loved you was a trick. Maybe he's just cruel. Is there something he has to gain from loving you? Maybe he hopes to take over your uncle's orchard someday." As if to punctuate his words, his large belly gurgled loudly in hunger.

Katiyana scrunched her eyebrows together, considering Jalb's words, confusion evident on her face.

"Enough of all this," Duan said. "Be considerate of the girl. Let's not upset her. And the soup is ready, after all."

Jalb rolled his eyes.

I watched with interest as they prepared the table. I wondered how Corto and Arrapato would sit and eat, but they managed fine. They arranged their stools close together and then slid in front of them, scooting their feet in coordinated baby steps. I imagine one had learned to use his right hand most often and the other his left. They climbed backward up the bracing bars of the tall stool simultaneously. While the stools around the fire accommodated little legs, the stools around the normal-sized table stood a little taller. I wondered why they didn't just saw a few inches off the legs of the table.

Kurz pulled a stool out for Katiyana, gesturing for her to sit down. When up on these stools, the little men sat closer to the same height as their guest. Even Pokole, who sat right on top of the table, could look the princess in the eye without tilting his head up.

Jalb ladled Katiyana's share first, filling her fired clay bowl to the brim. Although his chin cleared the table by only a few inches, he didn't spill a drop.

"Thank you," she said.

Jalb grunted.

"Don't let him scare you." Kapos leaned in close to the princess, his fine hair swaying toward her.

But Katiyana couldn't eat before voicing one more question. "Are the Simkins' really liars and thieves?"

"We don't need to talk about that right now, dear," Duan said.

"No, I think she should hear it." Kurz must have sensed Katiyana's uneasiness.

"Yeah, a story's better that Corto's bodily noises anyway," Jalb said.

"It's not me," Corto defended. "It's always Arrapato."

"Enough, you numbskulls!" Kurz yelled. "We have a lady in the house now."

Corto and Arrapato snickered quietly. Jalb rolled his eyes again.

Each dwarf spoke in turn, telling stories of their

encounters with the Simkins. A horribly poor family with too many children, they left a stinky reputation behind them wherever they went. You couldn't speak their name within fifty yards of the market without the sellers covering their goods for fear of them being stolen, according to the dwarves.

"And I've heard they never bathe," Kapos said. "Disgusting."

Katiyana laughed at that. "I don't remember Jeremy smelling like he never bathed." She thought for a moment. "I remember his smell, pleasant and woodsy."

"Go on," Duan encouraged.

"It's comforting now that I remember." She bowed her head and fiddled with her hands in her lap. Then she lifted her eyes suddenly before speaking again. "Until after all the sweaty work in the hot sun. Then I couldn't stand to be near him." She laughed, a glossy look covering her eyes; she remembered him fondly, as did I.

"The truth is," Kurz began. "Mr. and Mrs. Simkins are known as the laziest, fattest people in all of Mischief. Their children beg and steal for the family's living."

The dwarves began a debate about how many children actually lived in the Simkins' home.

"I know it's more than ten," offered Kurz.

"I heard fifteen," said Arrapato.

"I heard twenty-seven." This was the first time I had the pleasure of hearing Pokole speak. Oh, the surprise at hearing his high, squeaky voice! None of the other's voices would have given them away as being different, but the quality of Pokole's voice resembled that of a bird, or an exaggerating mother speaking to its babe.

"Pokole, don't be ridiculous, you nitwit," Kurz chuckled. "There's no such thing as having twenty-seven children."

Pokole gave a gentle shrug of his shoulders before carefully placing a spoon full of soup into his mouth.

Poor Katiyana. She looked more confused than ever. She watched the others eat for a time, her thoughts deep, her eyes vacant. I marveled at the contradiction between what Katiyana and I knew of Jeremy, and what the dwarves had reported. Eventually, the princess picked up her spoon and finally took a bite of Jalb's delicious-looking concoction. I wished I could smell it, and taste the onions, carrots, potatoes, and broth. The queen only allowed me to eat porridge.

"You don't want to go mixing up with a family like that," Kurz continued, now as serious as ever.

"And if that Simkins ever comes around here, I'll chop him up and put him in the next stew," said Jalb.

At that, Katiyana and most of the dwarves dropped their spoons and pushed their bowls away from them; only Corto and Arrapato continued to eat.

"What about all of you?" she asked. "Why do you live so far into the forest? And why was Kurz being sold as a slave?"

"It's a dangerous world for dwarves," Duan replied. "We live so deep in the forest to keep hidden. Some people who find us like to capture us and sell us into slavery. And in Mischief it's not against the law."

"Safer here than in Mayhem, though," Kurz said. "The queen of Mayhem has all dwarves killed as soon as they're discovered."

"That's awful," Katiyana said. "I can't believe anyone would want to kill such cute little men."

Jalb let out a grunt, and Kurz glared at Katiyana. "Don't be calling us cute," he warned.

"Or little," added Jalb.

"I'm sorry," said Katiyana, holding back a smirk. They were cute. And they were little. And they were men, after all. I couldn't help smiling myself, especially given their reaction.

Duan kept talking. "Corto and Arrapato have never been caught because nobody wants them. But people love to pay money to see them. They have a whole act they do at the market on occasion, but mostly we have everything we need here in the forest."

"And how did you come about this house?"

All the dwarves bowed their heads. "Mother Dwarf," Kurz said. "She was a dwarf whose parents actually kept and raised her. Most of the time, people who have dwarves abandon them or let them die. That's what happened to most of us. We were abandoned when we were children." All of the dwarves avoided looking at the princess, ashamed of their history. Kurz cleared his throat and continued. "Anyway, Mother Dwarf wasn't abandoned. She was kept, cherished, and loved. When her parents died, they left her this house. She took every one of us in, starting with Duan when he was only a babe."

"She'd have turned no one out," Duan said. "No one."

"What happened to her?" Katiyana queried.

"She got old," Kapos began to explain, but he stopped. It must have hurt to remember; all of the dwarves obviously had a huge love and respect for the woman.

"She died last spring," Kurz finished.

Jalb began clearing some of the dishes and preparing a pot of hot water to wash them. Then Duan called all of the dwarves away from the table to discuss something in secret. Kurz and Kapos followed him while Corto and Arrapato lifted Pokole into the air and placed him back on his small stool.

Katiyana watched Jalb dry dishes as he watched the others form a small circle around the fire and whisper.

When they finished, they faced Katiyana and Jalb. "We've decided to invite Kat to stay as long as she needs to," Duan said. "In honor of Mother Dwarf."

"In honor of Mother Dwarf," the rest echoed in unison as they bowed their heads once more.

"Nobody asked me," murmured Jalb.

"That's because the rest of us agreed and either way the majority rules," Kurz said, sounding annoyed at Jalb's persistent antagonizing.

I had hoped for this. I couldn't think of a better place for Katiyana than this safe and secret cottage.

Katiyana didn't seem so sure. "As long as I can leave whenever I need to." Perhaps she thought of Jeremy and hoped for his return.

"You're not the slave. I am, you stupid girl."

Katiyana smiled. She must have known by now—as did I—that Kurz only said such things to those he cared for most.

"She'll have to earn her keep," Jalb said, and I'm sure it was true. One more mouth to feed could send any humble household over the edge. "I may cook better than any woman and tidy things up impeccably, but sometimes I get tired of doing all the work myself."

"She can go to market," Kurz said. "She can take Corto and Arrapato to earn money and she can purchase things for us."

"We'll eat more bread than we've ever had before," said Duan, shaking his hands in excitement.

"And maybe some wine here and there," added Kurz.

"Yeah, and it's better than one of us going and risking being caught," Kapos reasoned. He turned to Katiyana to explain. "Kurz is the one who usually goes to market. But it's risky. He's been caught and sold into slavery at least ten times."

"More like fifty-seven," squeaked Pokole, and everyone laughed.

"It has not been fifty-seven times," defended Kurz amid his laughter. "You silly, breakable dwarf."

Katiyana looked to Jalb. "I'd be happy to go to market."

Jalb grunted.

"I also know how to bake bread using things we could purchase at the market. It would even save a little money. I don't know what a loaf of bread costs, but Jeremy always told me it cost less to buy flour than buy bread."

"Well, you shouldn't listen to any Simkins," he murmured.

"At my old home, I did all the cooking and washing. I know how to do it all. I'd be happy to help you as well."

Duan leaned in to Kurz. "She's good at bargaining too."

"Fine," relented Jalb. "But if that Simkins comes back, I'm going to give him a piece of my mind."

"Careful, Jalb. There isn't a lot to spare there," Pokole said, shaking his head.

Katiyana bit her lip, but when even Jalb chuckled at the tiniest dwarf, she let her laughter free.

A Glimpse

With Katiyana safely tucked away in the depths of Fluttering Forest, I turned my thoughts to Jeremy Simkins. When I wanted to see someone in particular, all I had to do was think of a person's name and an image materialized before me. I thought of Jeremy and there he was—sleeping and drooling all over the pillow he seemed to share with two other children.

I didn't know what to think of it. What important things needed to be taken care of? Sleeping under his own roof in the comfort of his own home? If you could call it comfort; I wouldn't. One of his siblings threw an elbow straight into his cheekbone as I looked on, forcing Jeremy to flinch and groan in his sleep.

He rose early in the morning, just as the sun began to give a hint of its existence by casting a far-off glow.

"Jeremy, where're yer goin'?" one of the small children asked, sitting up in the bed as Jeremy laced his boots. What long, ratted hair she had! Even in the dark I could tell it would take ages to comb through, the way it crawled out from her head. I guessed it was more from lack of attention than a night of tossing and turning. Five of them slept in the same tiny room.

"I have to go to work," he answered softly.

"Will yer be late again?" She rubbed her eye with her fist.

"Yes. It may even be a couple of days before I'm back."

The child perked up, dusting off any remaining sleepiness. "Will yer be goin' to the market? Will yer bring me somethint?" she begged with excitement.

Jeremy kissed her on the forehead. "Not this time. I'm sorry, Becky, but I can't spare any money right now. Mother and father need it all to take care of you."

"Well, will yer bring me a present then?"

Jeremy laughed at the sweet girl. I must say, the Simkins home was tolerable while everyone but these two slept.

He crept out of the room into the living area where more children slept. A woman cracked open the door of another room and peeked out. I remembered her as soon as I saw her, even though it had been years, and my peering into their home had been so brief. Her blunt, curly hair framed her fat face, and she wore a long nightgown that failed at hiding her innumerable lumpy curves. Cora Simkins. Dastardly woman.

"Don' eat any o' the food. I'll need it fer the li'l ones." By the looks of it, I thought, she would probably hog it all herself. "And don' ferget. If you don' bring back enough wages next time, don' bother comin' at all."

"Yes, ma'am," Jeremy said.

Father Simkins came and stood by his wife's side, creaking the door open wide. I struggled for his name. What was it?

"Isn' tha right, Bert?"

Tall, slender, and refusing to stand up for the boy, he seemed like just the sort of man to do whatever his wife said. "'Tis right."

Jeremy looked over the sleeping children and waved at Becky who had come out of her room to say good-bye. She rubbed both her eyes and yawned before waving back. "Good-bye, Jeremy. I'll miss yer."

"I'll miss you too."

"B'gone now," Cora grumbled. "Bes' not ta disturb her no more." She pulled a shawl tightly around her broad shoulders.

With a confident nod, Jeremy stepped out into the

damp of early morning. The sun remained in slumber, but a fraction of its coming warmth began to turn the frost on the grass into dew.

With the vast, level countryside of Mischief spread out before him, Jeremy set out, going who knows where. He hiked from farm to farm at a determined pace, asking for work. A farmer let him help dig an irrigation ditch in exchange for breakfast. But when the man learned Jeremy's last name, he ordered him off his land.

At the next farm, he found a woman harvesting the last of her pumpkin patch. She knelt on the ground, cutting the stems off the vine.

"Excuse me, ma'am," Jeremy called out from the edge of her field of leafy green. "Would you have any work? I'm looking to be hired on, but I'll take even an hour's work if you have any." He spoke with earnest, shaking his head with feeling as he twisted his hat in his hand. Sweat dripped from the ends of his hair. How desperate he looked. I wished I could help him somehow.

The woman paused—setting down her knife—and sauntered closer. "And who might you be?" she inquired.

He looked her in the eye. "My name's Jeremy."

She put her hands on her hips. The faded floral dress she wore flapped in the breeze, as did the clothes hanging from a rope in the distance. "Jeremy what?"

She sounded like the type of woman never to be trifled with.

"Jeremy Simkins." He kept his gaze on her, even if a look of doubt came across his once hopeful face. Hopeful, but not foolish. I don't think it surprised him when she kindly but firmly asked him to be on his way.

And so it went up and down the southernmost countryside of Mischief. I began to realize the most discouraging thing for anyone to endure is having the last name Simkins. One chubby woman ran after him as she waved a rolling pin, screaming, "You'd better get off my farm before my husband gets back or he'll kill you!" One man threw his fist into Jeremy's eye, landing him face down in a mixture of mud and hog slop. "That's for the hay you Simkinses stole from me last year."

"I've never stolen anything before," Jeremy spat through a face full of filth.

The man kicked at Jeremy, his heavy boot catching him in the thigh before he scrambled out of range. "Get off my farm. And don't ever come back."

Bruised and discouraged, Jeremy trudged on until he came upon a line of trees shading a clear, pebbled stream. Gingerly, he knelt in the green growth by the water and washed as best he could, applying the cool liquid carefully to his sunburned skin. After slurping several handfuls of water, and resting for a brief moment, Jeremy headed toward town and Mischief Market. And what do you know? He hustled straight to the north platform where I guessed he would be looking for a man named Juno.

The same man who had sold Kurz to Katiyana stood on the platform before a small crowd, auctioning a collection of silverware.

"It's the finest silver, to be sure," he called.

A woman in the crowd began the bidding at seven silver coins.

"Now don't be insulting," Juno roared back. "This is pure silver, through and through." He picked up a fork and bit down on it, pretending to break a tooth. His antics brought a ripple of sporadic chuckling from his audience.

"I'll bid five doces," a man shouted.

"Now that's more like it!" Juno exclaimed "And we have five doces, a bidder willing to give five doces, and who will beat it?"

Jeremy stood back, appraising the crowd and waiting for his chance.

"All right then. For five doces from you, my fine gent, and here's your silver." He closed the lid on the rectangular wooden box.

The winning bidder moved up the steps of the platform to pay for his treasure.

"Here you are, sir." Juno hefted the weight of the man's silver in his hand before tucking the coins expertly into a hidden pocket at his waist. As he handed the box of silverware over, his eyes caught Jeremy's earnest expression over the heads of the crowd. "Um, excuse me ladies and gentleman," he began as he scooted toward the platform stairs. "I will be taking a short break. But don't go far, I've many more treasures to tempt and please every last one of you!" As if released from a spell, the crowd began to disperse or chat idly.

Jeremy approached the platform. "Sorry, my friend."

"Oh, that's all right. They'll come back. And what might Jeremy Simkins be doing here?" He looked past his friend. "I don't see your apple cart."

"I've lost my job at the orchard."

Juno moved in close and whispered. "You have? What are you going to do?"

"I've been looking for new work. I'm sure I'll find something soon." Jeremy gave him a reassuring smile. "But if you hear of anything, you'll let me know?"

"Of course I will, old friend." He slapped Jeremy on the shoulder.

"Juno, there's one more thing."

"What is it?"

"Has a girl been to see you? A dark haired girl named Kat? She's a friend of mine and I told her that if she came to you and mentioned my name you'd help her find lodging."

Juno looked upward as if seeking divine inspiration. "No, not that I recall."

"Are you sure?"

"Yeah, I'm sure. I think I'd remember someone throwing the name Simkins around." He smiled, wide and carefree.

A puzzled look crept across Jeremy's face.

"Will you be all right?" Juno asked.

"Oh yes, I'm sure I will." But for the first time ever, I noticed that the boy lacked confidence in his words and expression. I think it unnerved him greatly that Katiyana had not been to see Juno.

Juno must have picked up on the change as well. He reached into his pocket. "Here. I earned this pair of doces just yesterday selling a dwarf slave."

Jeremy accepted the money. "Thank you, friend. This will get me through the next week or so." He turned to leave. "Remember to let me know if you hear of any work."

"Will do, Jeremy. Will do." He waddled his large body back to the center of the platform, calling out boisterously for spectators and potential buyers to return.

Jeremy slipped the money into his trouser pocket. Moving quickly through town, he took the road to Barney's orchard this time, avoiding Fluttering Forest to his left and the span of farmland to his right.

He took long, quick strides away from town,

reaching the orchard well before sundown. Under the trees, he slowed to a stroll, choosing out a shiny red apple from a low-hanging branch. He munched hungrily, savoring every bite. Then he ate another one.

Jeremy wandered toward the house, retracing the grounds he and Katiyana had worked for so many years. The land around him rested in total stillness, as though it mourned the loss of its caretakers. Passing the house, Jeremy peeked into the barn. Even the animals rested quietly. Feed had been freshly spread for them, suggesting to me that Barney worked on alone or had already hired someone new. But watching Jeremy's face struggle through a range of emotion, from confusion to wide-eyed alarm and back, I guessed that Jeremy wondered if Katiyana had left at all.

Finally, quietly, he entered the house, stepping cautiously through the door to avoid its usual creak.

The dark house felt empty to me, though the soft rumble of snores alerted Jeremy to Barney's sleeping form, slumped in the dusty old rocking chair. On tiptoe, Jeremy searched through the little house, seeing, as I did, no sign of Katiyana. Or of anyone else, for that matter. Descending back into the front room, Jeremy paused and stared at Barney a moment, the final echoes of sunlight casting rays on the unshaven face, the ragged clothing. What a pitiful creature. I mean Barney, not Jeremy.

"Is someone there?" Barney asked suddenly, his head still resting against the rocking chair.

Jeremy stiffened, holding his breath.

"Is that you, girl?" Barney sat up straight, the wooden chair creaking loudly in protest, and listened intently. When nobody answered, he covered his face with his hands and began to weep, a response that could have broken even the hardest heart. "What have I done?" he moaned, his shoulders shaking with sobs. "What have I done?"

Under the cover of his cries, Jeremy quickly crept back out the door, latching it silently behind him.

❧ ❋ ❧

The next morning, Jeremy woke up on the ground in Barney's barn. Hay lay scattered all around him and stuck to his clothing and hair. As Jeremy woke to the sound of bleating and pecking, Barney entered the barn, feeling his way along the wall toward the animal feed. He managed well enough, I mused, even without the benefit of his sight. I wondered why he'd been so lazy over the years. How much it had cost him!

Jeremy froze, trying not to rustle in the scratchy hay, but Barney stopped as he bent down to scoop chicken feed. "Is someone there?" he called out.

Jeremy held his breath, willing himself into

complete silence, and Barney soon resumed his chores. As soon as he finished and had returned to the house, Jeremy gathered his small pack and thin jacket, secured the barn door behind him, and left the way he'd come, his eyes sending a silent farewell to the trees that held so many memories.

Being out of other options, I suppose, Jeremy went home. With the aid of daylight, I began to remember what made the Simkins' home so awful. The Simkins family lived in a home much too small for two adults and thirteen children. The outside and inside needed repair; one window tilted to the side and constantly let in a breeze. The inside walls were splattered with crusty food stains that probably dated back to when the first Simkins child began walking about with sticky fingers.

Jeremy looked to be the eldest, but not by far. And what a noise came from the house! All of the younger children greeted him with smiles and giggles. It didn't surprise me given his interaction with Becky two nights before; he must have been just as sweet with all of them given their obvious adoration.

It appeared their clothing came from old curtains or bed sheets. The hair of one little girl formed a ratted ball on top of her head and two of the other children's noses constantly produced a greenish gunk.

"D'yer bring a present?" Becky asked.

Jeremy, who had looked forlorn the entire way

from Barney's, picked the child up and produced a weary looking smile. "I've brought something even better than a present," he told her as he swung her around and straddled her on his side. Becky giggled with delight, her laughter true and charming. She had a scraped knee, and her ratted hair stuck out in all directions. He pulled the two doces from his pocket and offered them to the little girl in a shabby dress. "Give those to the lady of the house, will you?"

"I'm the la'y of the house!" Becky shouted happily.

"Oh, right. I forgot. Well, give it to your mother. She'll know just what to do with it." Jeremy tweaked her nose and then set her back down.

When Cora Simkins saw the glint of money in her young daughter's grubby hand, a wide grin nearly split her face in two.

"Where'd yer get this?" she asked Becky.

"Jeremy brough' it. 'E said yer'd know just what to do with it."

Cora sat at the table and turned away from the cornbread dripping with butter in her hands to look at Jeremy, who stood quietly in the doorway. "So yer've earned another couple o' weeks. Have yer taken to stealin' like the others?"

Jeremy glared at her as he twisted the brim of his hat in his hands. He looked thoroughly annoyed. "No."

"Shame," Cora said through a mouthful of food.

The shuffling of grass out in the yard caught Jeremy's attention, and he moved to the window.

"Here come yer brothers, Becky," Cora said. "Open the door. I'm sure they've brought somethint grand. Oh, we'll feast tonight."

Jeremy went outside to head them off. "What have you been doing?"

"Nothin'," the tallest boy said.

"Empty your pockets."

The three tall, lanky boys obeyed. An array of money and other valuables appeared in their hands.

"How many times have I told you not to steal? Nobody will ever think any better of you if you keep on like this."

"But she makes us," the shortest of the three protested. Perhaps, to some, this might seem a weak defense. But what is a child to do when their own mother encourages them to steal? I imagined, from Cora Simkins, it was more than encouraged— required, is more like it.

"Have yer found a job yet?" one of the boys challenged.

"Not yet."

"I heard Farmer Haskel's lookin' fer help in the spring."

I wasn't familiar with the name Haskel.

"That's too late. I need something now."

"Yer not goin' ta find anythin' in the winter."

Jeremy looked out across the field, his face hopeful, determined, even expectant. With those far-away eyes, I wondered if he was thinking of Katiyana. Did he expect her to come walking out of the horizon? "I can't wait that long."

Cora called the boys inside. "Well, what're yer still doing here?" she demanded when she saw Jeremy. "Shouldn' yer be out looking fer more work? Two doces goes by fast in a house with so many mouths ta feed."

Although Cora's prodding got his feet moving once again, I imagined Jeremy was thinking only of one mouth—the mouth that he had kissed a few days before, the mouth that he had lost.

Winter

After watching Jeremy for two whole days, I knew little more than I had before, except he was trying to find a way to earn money and giving it all to the greedy Cora Simkins. Not much of a hero if you ask me, but I decided to withhold judgment long enough to see how things played out. In the meantime, I decided seven dwarves were the best chance I had for entertainment. And I longed to watch the princess interact with her new friends.

I had every confidence that Princess Katiyana would win over each and every dwarf in no time at all. But Jalb continued to resist her charm. There he sat, watching with disbelieving eyes as Katiyana kneaded bread. "There's no way it will taste as good as the bread we buy at market. And how can paying a copper coin for flour make it less expensive than paying a grumpet for a loaf?"

"We've told you," Corto said. "A sack of flour will make fifty loaves of bread."

"Yeah, stop your complaining and let the girl work in peace," added Arrapato.

Jalb pushed away from the table, knocked over his stool, and waddled with his stubby legs out the door, slamming it behind him. I marveled at how his masculine features and moody temperament starkly contrasted with his domestic skills.

Katiyana's face sank into a look of disappointment, but her hands never stopped working the heavy dough.

After rising and baking to a perfect golden brown, the loaves were left to cool before being cut and spread with globs of Jalb's own wild raspberry preserves. When Jalb came back inside, he resisted having a slice, although I'm pretty sure I noticed his mouth watering. But when he learned Katiyana had purchased the flour with her own money, he apologized for being leery and ate almost half a loaf himself.

"I'm sorry, Kat. I didn't know you had any money."

"Well, I have plenty. And I'd be happy to pay for my little spot on the floor by the fire as well. It only seems fair."

"You don't have to do that," Kurz said, glaring at Jalb. "Remember Mother Dwarf," he whispered as he elbowed him.

"Well, I'm the best cook in all of Mischief," Jalb began. "But I've never been much of a baker. If Kat can provide us with bread, I see no reason why she should have to pay anything more for a spot of ground."

"Thank you," Katiyana said with a single nod of her head.

Over the next few days I watched each dwarf seek Katiyana's attention and good opinion. Kurz and Duan spoke to her with kindness and complimented her on everything. "Well done," Duan said every time he ate a piece of Katiyana's bread. "You're a wonder," Kurz told her as she carefully and thoroughly swept the floor. "How did we ever do without you?" That one brought a grunt from Jalb.

I imagined saying such things to the princess myself, if I had the privilege of interacting with her. How I would have enjoyed that opportunity! I also watched them as they performed small acts of kindness, the kind I like to think I would have done as well.

Kapos collected cotton and feathers until he had enough to make a soft pillow for the princess. Corto and Arrapato never ceased trying to make the princess laugh. Jalb always invited her to work with him when vegetables needed to be chopped or dirty dishes lay about. But none of them received her affections so completely and readily as Pokole. Right from the start, the two were inseparable.

Katiyana even let him travel to the market with her. She carried him on her hip disguised as a child.

Kurz argued. "It's too dangerous. He could get hurt by any number of careless, stupid people. Besides, he's fifteen years old—he doesn't want you carrying him around like a baby."

"Yes, I do," Pokole said.

Katiyana laughed. "Well, that settles it, doesn't it?" She gave Kurz a kind, reassuring look. "I'll take good care of him."

And she kept her promise. She carried Pokole the entire way, walked with great care, and showed him all the delights of the market, all the things that still captivated her attention as well.

On her first trip to the market with Pokole on her side, the princess learned not to ask around for Jeremy Simkins. What the dwarves had told her was true, and mentioning his name limited where she could shop, since the two men she asked that day forbade her from ever coming back. And she avoided Juno altogether as well.

But there were many other shops and sights at the market to distract her from thinking about Jeremy Simkins. Katiyana, as Duan had said, really could bargain. I watched with pride as she remarked on vegetables being too rotten or prices being too high. But she always treated people with kindness and respect. She soon became known by many of the market sellers as a regular customer as long as they treated her with fairness. It brought me joy to watch as she greeted them with confidence, remembering their names and past conversations. And her compassion! If someone struggled, say, with pushing their cart or juggling their children, Katiyana offered help before any other.

Many of these trips were special favors to Pokole; she never brought him with her when she had to take Corto and Arrapato for a show or when she would have to carry back a sack of flour.

Although I sometimes found my thoughts wandering to what may yet be in store for Katiyana, the only thing I cared about at that time was that she was busy and happy, making important discoveries about the world and about herself, all while tucked away in a safe place. Maybe she'd live with the dwarves forever, or maybe she'd marry Jeremy or some other young man. Even if I had to stay in the mirror permanently, I could bear it as long as Katiyana stayed happy and alive.

The days with her seven little men turned to weeks, and weeks turned to months. The thin, crisp autumn air turned into stiff winter chill. Katiyana stopped going to Mischief Market, having stored enough flour and other supplies to last them until spring, and the eight of them hid away inside their small, one-room cottage.

Only Jalb left regularly now, mostly to get away

from the others and have some peace and quiet, if only for a minute. At least, that's what he mumbled every time he walked out the door. Corto, Arrapato, and Kapos tried to come up with some magic or acrobatic tricks to try at the market in spring; they made the most comical human pyramid. They even got Kurz to try a magic trick with them. It involved trying to make a crowd believe Corto and Arrapato had actually been separated by a knife while inside a box. But Kapos and Kurz could not easily be made to look enough like the brothers to fool a crowd, except maybe from a great distance. But their efforts kept Katiyana and the rest of the dwarves—not to mention myself—entertained for hours upon hours.

Katiyana helped dispel the winter blues as well, reading stories by the short-reaching heat of the fire. She had bought several books at the market and begun a small collection.

I'll paraphrase one of the stories the best I can, because I think it made her realize for the first time that Jeremy may never come back.

There had once been a little girl, the story began. She wore her hair in pigtails and carted about a doll whose own hair was made of red yarn. The girl's only playmate was a selfish boy who loved to steal the doll and hide it for fun. Only the girl did not think it was fun. The boy secretly loved the girl, but didn't know how to tell her. They grew older, and the boy had to go away for a time. He had places to see and things he wanted to do. First he had an adventure at sea, where he narrowly escaped an angry crew of sailors because he had stowed away. But they spared his life and allowed him to work on the ship. The boy saw so many places on his sea adventures, but loved none so much as a place far in the east where men and women both wore dresses and shaved their heads. He stayed while his ship went on. Then he put on a dress, shaved his head, and went to war for the foreign country, fighting enemies with a jagged sword. All this time, the boy wrote letters to his childhood playmate—letters that he never sent. Finally, the war ended and the boy was named a governor over many regions for his faithful service in the army. He could not refuse, and filled his duty with wisdom and love for the people of his newfound home. But there was the girl, always in his thoughts and plans, until one day he could not stand to be away from her any longer. He again boarded a ship and returned to the land of his birth at last. When he found his childhood playmate, she lay in a sickbed, aged and alone. Too far had he traveled; too long had he waited. She died shortly after his arrival.

"Well, that's depressing," Kurz said once Katiyana had finished telling it. "You made Pokole cry. And Jalb couldn't even listen to the whole thing; he's been outside for most of it."

Katiyana hung her head, her face sorrowful, and her thoughts quiet and distant.

"Well, I thought it was charming," Duan reassured. "And beautifully read."

Katiyana smiled in appreciation.

"Yeah, and I didn't cry!" Pokole yelled in his high-pitched voice, masking his emotions. "It's just the onions Jalb cut up earlier."

Kapos stood up and kissed Katiyana on the cheek. "Thank you for the story," he said. "It was beautiful." He glared at Kurz.

"What?" Kurz asked. "Wasn't that the most depressing story you've ever heard? I think I'm going to find a nice dark hole to crawl into and cry myself to sleep tonight."

Everyone pulled away from the fire to move about the room except for Katiyana and Kurz.

The dwarf studied the princess. "What's bothering you? Besides how miserable that story was?"

"Hmmm?" Katiyana asked, pulling her eyes out of their inward focus.

"What's bothering you?"

"Oh, nothing, I just . . ."

"You can tell me."

I found his fatherly sincerity touching.

Katiyana rubbed her fingers across the front cover of the book. "I can't stop wondering about Jeremy Simkins."

"Because of the story?"

Katiyana nodded.

"What is it about the story that makes you think of Jeremy?"

Katiyana looked Kurz in the eye. "What if he comes back too late?"

"I don't know," Kurz said, leaning closer to the princess and resting his elbows on his thighs. "How late is too late?"

"I don't know."

"I'd like to hug you right now, but it's awkward for me being so much shorter." Kurz smiled, and I wondered if he was just trying to make the princess smile as well. If that's what he aimed for, he succeeded.

Katiyana scooted her stool next to Kurz's and stooped down so their heads came to the same height. She leaned onto him, placing her head on his shoulder. Kurz held his little arm across her back and patted.

"Listen," Kurz whispered, and by now several of the dwarves looked on. "Either he comes back, or you figure out how long is too long and move forward. Understand?"

The princess nodded, her face scrunching Kurz's white shirt as she moved.

Jalb came back inside, shivering despite the fact that he had plenty of clothing and body fat to keep a man warm on a mild winter's evening. "Time to cook dinner," he said.

Katiyana stood up. "I'll help you, Jalb."

"That's all right," he said, closing the door. He began selecting carrots and potatoes from a barrel in the corner of the room and muttered, "I don't care if I hear another story for the rest of my life."

While it brought me joy to see Katiyana doing so well, especially considering all that she'd been through, my heart ached for her company after her conversation with Kurz. Though I'd watched the girl closely over the years, she had never borne her soul to me the way she had to her caring little dwarf. Perhaps she never would. How unfair! It wasn't often that I fell beneath the weight of despair, but in that moment I couldn't block it out. I longed to be free. And more than anything else, I wanted to be a part of Katiyana's life.

I shut off my thoughts after that, and the vision of the princess and her little men faded away until I sat alone in my black existence. I wiped a tear off my face and waited for time to ease the dispirited feelings of my soul.

$$\text{꙳ ✳ ꙳}$$

To prepare you for what's coming, I'll explain that I had to be careful when I watched the princess; the queen of Mayhem consulted me often, and she could see whatever I looked at. My painstaking efforts over the years to keep the princess a secret had worked thus far. I would continue to watch with care, but sometimes trying to avoid catastrophe only ensures that you'll get it anyway.

Queen Radiance

In order to tell the story of how I got in the mirror, I'll have to include the queen of Mayhem. I hate to do something so unpleasant, but as I said in the beginning, this story is also about a queen.

Born Tirnosha (which means "cruel" in the language of the forefathers of Mayhem), she grew strong-willed and powerful in speech. Her parents died in her youth, and the viciousness of her rule began far too soon.

I knew little about it, other than what I had heard in town gossip. But the things I heard frightened me: implementing torture to enforce new laws, beheading servants who displeased her, burning the homes of those who could not pay taxes. I vowed to keep my distance; given the location of my home—dozens of miles from the castle and in the outskirts of Fluttering Forest—I thought this would be easy.

I still remember the day she came to my door; fear rose up within me when I saw her face. I knew her immediately, though I'd never seen her before. Her crown rested atop her head, colorful jewels fixed inside pure, thin gold. She wore a long, slender black dress, with sleeves to her wrists—the tops fitting to her arms, then spreading wide at the elbow, as if each arm wore its own billowing dress. The bodice framed her chest tightly, forcing me to pay attention to the shape of her body.

I had heard of her devastating beauty, but never could I have imagined the figure before me. Her long, dark hair fell past her shoulders in soft curls. Her dark eyes penetrated mine, awakening something inside of me. Of course it pleased me to look at her, but real beauty is not something that can be seen with the eyes. Knowing the queen's true character, I resolved not to let her appearance affect me.

"Q-q-queen Rad-d-diance," I foolishly stammered. By this time she had changed her name to Queen Radiance—a little presumptuous, and certainly deceiving, but perhaps an improvement from Tirnosha. "What can I do for you?"

"May I enter?" If her looks hadn't been enough, her voice lured me in, lower in pitch than I expected, pleasant and smooth. For a moment it felt the same as watching a brewing thunderstorm, as if something both dangerous and exciting was lurking behind the clouds.

"Yes, of course." I opened the door wide to welcome her.

She gave a nod to her driver and guards, waiting in the royal carriage. She then stepped into my tiny cottage, lifting the hem of her dress, allowing me to sneak a glance at her sleek ankles.

I cleared my throat. "Can I offer you some tea?"

"Yes, please," she answered as she scrutinized the room.

I pulled a chair out from the table and helped her sit down. Then I poured water from the kettle and made her my favorite rosemary and lemon tea.

She accepted the cup with her long fingers and sipped delicately.

As she slowly drank every last drop, I wondered why she had come. The suspense tormented me.

When she finished, she placed the cup down on the table and looked at me with those horribly irresistible eyes. "I hear you are skilled in sorcery," she hinted.

"Oh, um . . ." I stammered, reaching for the teapot and refilling her cup with shaky hands. What would someone so cruel do with knowledge of sorcery? Destroy everything. A sorceress queen—I knew the dangers, the limitless powers. I determined to be strong.

"I do," I admitted, slumping into the chair across from her and filling a cup of my own. "My father taught me, and his father taught him."

"Are they dead?" she asked. "Your father and your grandfather?"

"Yes."

"You are like me then—young and alone." A look of true sorrow covered her face, dampening the power of her eyes.

"I suppose."

"You have a duty to your queen. Your kingdom."

I disagreed, but I wasn't about to tell her that.

"I need you to teach me the art of magic."

"The art of magic can't be learned by just anyone," I lied. The truth was, anyone willing enough could learn.

I had lived in Fluttering Forest all my years, living the simple life of a sorcerer and learning the skills that had been handed down for generations. I had only ever used my knowledge for medicinal reasons. I knew the delicate practices of magic. When used for good, they can be controlled, but only if they are respected and feared. When used for selfishness or power seeking, they are dangerous beyond reason, unfathomably devastating. I didn't want the queen to learn.

"How do we know unless we try?" she questioned. All of my previous determination to resist her charms melted when I saw her wide, joyful smile. It weakened me instantly. My knees got hot and before I could help myself, I felt a smile form on my face in response.

Still, I knew there were some things the queen of Mayhem should never know. "I'll teach you the theory of spells," I compromised.

"Spells?"

"Yes." I knew that I had to convince her that spells were adequate. "Spells are useful no matter where you are or what you're doing. And they're powerful."

"That's a good place to start," she said. "I'll be back tomorrow."

I watched her drive away, trying to think of a way to escape her. But at the same time, I couldn't wait to see her again.

For the next few weeks she came, every day, and unfortunately she excelled at the craft.

"Amazing, Queen Radiance," I praised when her first spell caused a purple wildflower to grow right in the middle of my kitchen table.

Her talent caught me by surprise, and I found myself encouraging her. It felt good to have such a successful student. I had never taught anyone before and had never dreamed how satisfying it would be. "Don't think about the words too much," I instructed. "Let them flow freely from your tongue." I circled the table where she practiced, coaching her on. "Think of the spell you're creating. Ask it to come to life. What's in your heart and mind is more important than the words you speak."

I hate to admit it, but she enthralled me, and in only two moons, her skills surpassed mine. I looked forward to her coming every day and defended her name to those who suffered at her hand. Looking back, I'm convinced she put spells on me. I even came to believe I loved her.

Then one day a knock interrupted our spell session.

"Oh, I'm sure that's Fredrick," she said.

"Who's Fredrick?" I asked, intrigued. Nobody had ever come to the door during one of our sessions before.

"You haven't heard?" she asked. "Fredrick is my cousin. My parents arranged our marriage long ago, giving his family a small farm in the village of Costner in exchange for the match. He's nothing but a commoner now, but he's to be the next king of Mayhem."

"So he can't rule?"

"Only as my husband. If I were to die, he would lose his title."

I couldn't bear the thought of her dying (not back then), or the thought of her marrying Fredrick. She must have seen my despair.

"You're white as snow," she remarked. "Is anything wrong?"

I shook my head before answering the door.

Fredrick may have been a commoner, the son of a farmer, but he looked like royalty. He stood a full head above me, with broad shoulders, a straight back, and a confident but kind presence, his eyes the same green as ivy leaves.

"Fredrick, you look stunning," the queen said.

He looked past me to thank her and return the compliment. "And you must be her teacher," he said to me, reaching out his hand.

I accepted, and marveled at the warmth and strength of his fingers.

"Are you ready, Tirnosha?" he asked. I thought it strange that he called her by her real name.

The queen ceremoniously gathered her robe and pointed velvet shoes—she always removed these upon entering the cottage—and whispered something in Fredrick's ear. They looked into each other's eyes, smiling about her secret. If I had known then what kind of man Fredrick was, I could have avoided hating him.

But perhaps I should have suspected then that Queen Radiance sought to make me jealous in order to use and manipulate me. She didn't come back for four weeks.

When she finally returned one rainy afternoon, her red puffy eyes gave away her distress. "Jasper," she said. (How silly that I'm just barely telling you my name; I should have done that long ago.) "I need a spell. A powerful spell."

"Queen Radiance, you know spells better than I do. Why do you need me to help you with a spell?" I kept calm, masking the reality of my emotions. How I had longed to see her! What joy and excitement it brought me to find her once again at my door! And what angst it caused to see her in despair.

"Fredrick." She held back the tears.

"What is the matter with Fredrick? Is he sick?" The queen and I had not yet explored spells for medical use, and I stood ready to help if needed.

"He doesn't love me," she blurted, sobbing into her black-and-white embroidered handkerchief.

"Come in," I said, placing my hand on her shoulder. She moved into my embrace. I comforted her, held her, and welcomed her need for consolation. I thoroughly enjoyed her company over the next several days as she sent the royal carriage off and stayed with me in my cozy cottage, offering me all of her affections.

"I don't have to marry Fredrick," she told me. "It was my parent's wish, but by law I may choose whomever I please."

"You please me," I said. I know now what a stupid line that was, and gag at the thought of ever having said it to her, but remember, I thought I loved her.

She flattered me, stood by me as I cooked poached

eggs, laughed with me, and gave me every reason to believe we shared feelings of love and adoration. Then one morning, her plan to learn more about the practice of magic began to surface.

"I'm ready to move past spells," she said between sips of tea.

"What do you mean?" I asked.

"There is more to learn, isn't there? About sorcery?"

Queen Radiance wanted to learn the darker levels of magic, like fortune telling, mind reading, and looking into the future. I wanted to refuse, knowing she'd already used her talent for spells to adjust the weather, to punish less-than-perfect servants by giving them some plague or disease; she had even experimented on herself, casting spells to preserve her youthful vitality and accentuate her beauty. But at the same time, I longed to give her what she wanted. Becoming the king of Mayhem had little appeal, but the irresistible exquisiteness sitting before me . . . You must realize what a position this put me in.

"Have I ever shown you the magic mirror my father left me?"

"No," she answered, raising her eyebrows in interest.

I grew nervous; if she fell for the distraction, the ruin of Mayhem could be prolonged. If she didn't, our romance would certainly be over and possibly my life.

I retrieved the mirror from its hiding place beneath my bed and showed it to the queen.

"Why, it's just a hand mirror."

"Yes," I agreed. "But it's powerful. I think it could be the next step for you. It may be all you ever need."

"How does it work?" she asked, peering inside as she tucked a stray lock of shiny black hair behind her ear.

"All you do is step inside. Would you like to see?" I placed the mirror down on the table and held my hand out, beckoning her to come with me.

Her cold hand clasped mine and together we approached the surface of the mirror. As soon as our hands reached out and touched the glass, it sucked us inward until we landed in the small, dark enclosure.

"Now what?" she asked, looking around. "Do we get out the same way we came in?"

"Yes." The uneasiness in my gut began to take over the silly feelings of lust I had experienced in the days and weeks before. "Unless a spell is used to trap someone inside."

"But what good is that?" she asked. "Can it be used as a sort of prison?"

"Well, yes," I said. "But the mirror's much too valuable for that."

"What else can it do?" she inquired.

"Think of someone," I said. "Or something or somewhere."

The queen closed her eyes, and I knew instantly she had thought of Fredrick because an image of him came up on the small glass surface that acted as both entrance and exit to the mirror.

"What's he doing?" I wondered aloud.

Queen Radiance opened her eyes to see for herself. She moved closer and squinted at the image. "He's making a head wreath."

I laughed. "Is he going to wear it?"

She looked at me, suddenly grave. "Stay here," she said, before kissing me long on the lips. "I have a surprise for you." Her hand reached out for escape, and she slipped away from me, leaving the faint scent of her floral perfume—lilacs, I believe.

I watched speechless as she spoke these words, calling to life the spell that would entrap me.

"Mirror, Mirror, in my hand
Lock your door; enslave this man.
Ensure his lips speak only truth;
Keep lies behind tongue and tooth.
Hold him there, no longer free
Until death take him or me."

Frantic, only realizing what she had done after the spell was completed, I reached out my hand towards the smooth glass.

Nothing. I was trapped.

The queen of Mayhem married her cousin, Fredrick the commoner—son of Fredrick Baer and Alisa Whyte Baer—two days later. Then she wreaked even greater havoc throughout the kingdom, continuing the philosophy to rule with absolute power and tyranny. She brought many to their knees in fearful subservience, and she did it with ease, because, as I said before, there was no beauty inside of her. And I played a part in it all. Whenever the queen needed to locate someone, or whenever she sought to spy on one of her subjects, she came to me. The biggest regret of my life is that her outward appearance ever blinded me to the terror beneath.

Sharing the Mirror

Life inside the mirror was unpleasant at best, and downright depressing at worst. Queen Radiance kept the mirror in her private bedchambers; even during her marriage to King Fredrick I was kept from his view. He resided solely in a different part of the castle and was forbidden to enter the queen's dwelling. The mirror rested on top of her vanity, so she had easy access to see the things I could see. Lucky for me, her vanity rested in the path of streaming sunlight from her window; I'm sure I would have gone mad without that little bit of brightness every day.

As I've said before, to access a vision, I had only to think of a person or place specifically. I could see the queen whenever I wanted, but watching her made

me sick. Occasionally, I looked upon my old home—
which had since been occupied by a large family—
or some old acquaintances, wondering if they had
missed me. Much of the time I watched over the vil-
lages of Mayhem. I sorrowed for their inhabitants,
and I was amazed that even under such a queen they
found ways to laugh. By far my greatest interest over
all those years had been Princess Katiyana. But these
are the things I looked at only in the absence of the
queen.

She used me often. It made me feel awful to know
I'd been the instrument to so much ill will and destruction. "Show me the village of Ramuse," she would
say, and if anything looked awry she would send a
band of soldiers to set it right, either by fire or intimidating abuse. "Show me Tenser Waller," she would
say, and if the man or woman she asked to see looked
to be a traitor, well, she would take care of it in one
way or another. I'd seen more murders than I care to
remember, more pain, more tears, more blood. People
talked all over the kingdom of Mayhem, wondering
how the queen always knew if someone committed a
crime or quarreled or threatened an uprising against
her. Every attempt at freedom from her oppression
was easily and quickly silenced. And it was all because
of me and my foolishness.

She also watched the kingdom of Mischief with
vigilance, since its king and queen had tested her

patience early in her rule by playing practical jokes on their neighboring kingdom. Their efforts at friendly frivolity were returned with raging war. And even though the king and queen of Mischief had kept a fearful distance for some number of years, Queen Radiance wanted to be confident in their intentions toward her, or rather, in their fear of her. She asked to see them at least once a week.

Let me just explain one more thing. The queen provided me with a servant—several over the years, actually, since the queen often got rid of them for one reason or another—who came into my little mirror several times a day to bring me food and take care of anything else I needed. I watched with care, and listened, always turning off the power of the mirror in time for these predictable visits. None of these servants ever asked me how I felt about being locked inside a mirror, or how it was I came to be there, or how they could get me out. But it didn't matter. No servant would have risked the wrath of Queen Radiance to set free a strange sorcerer. They all did what they were told.

As I said, the servant visits were expected, but I couldn't always tell when the queen would be coming for information.

One day she asked me to show her the road to Mischief. I still remember how bright it was with the snow on the ground and the sun burning high.

On the road, two men stood, discussing whether to ask the kingdom of Mischief to interfere with the troubles found in Mayhem and the tyranny of Queen Radiance. I thought it strange they met on the road in the dead of winter. Perhaps one man lived in Mischief and the other in Mayhem, and the road served as their meeting place. Both had walked, and both looked frozen despite the shining sun. Fresh snow dappled the surrounding pine trees.

They whispered, and one in particular kept glancing around, paranoid they were being watched. How ironic, for I knew however carefully he watched, he would never be able to find me.

"We've got to do something," one said.

"But the queen will find out," the other said.

"Yes, she will," Queen Radiance interjected.

"Be quiet," I commanded. "You know I can't concentrate when you start talking on top of everything else." Lying to Queen Radiance had become a natural habit. To tell the truth, I simply couldn't stand the sound of her voice and told her it affected my concentration. I would say just about anything to get her to shut up.

After viewing their conversation—which ended in a decision to get more support, and hopefully from someone in the queen's army—she set off immediately, located her royal executioner, and called for her carriage. I feared for the men; Queen Radiance rarely went to deal with her subjects personally, and when she did . . . I shivered thinking about it. I watched through the mirror as she walked down the front steps of the castle in her stunning black and blue dress—her armored executioner close behind—and stepped into her carriage. "Drive on," she said as she put on her black, lace gloves. Her latest driver threw the reins up in the air and clapped them back down again, sending the carriage forward with a jolt.

I craved distraction. Feeling safe from her attentive eyes, and knowing my servant would not be in for two hours, I thought of Princess Katiyana and her seven little men. Really, it was the best entertainment to be had with stories and magic tricks and Pokole's funny remarks.

On this particular day, things in the dwarf house were relatively quiet, as if the bleakness of winter had finally engulfed them in its cloud. Katiyana sat on a low stool, her head resting against the brick wall and a book in her hand; Corto and Arrapato slept in front of the fire—how uncomfortable they looked stuck together while trying to sleep; Jalb sat at the table as if considering what to make for dinner but not wanting to begin yet; Pokole sat on top of the table, half-heartedly playing at a game on his own; the others sat around in silence.

Perhaps each thought about their own troubles and the unfairness life had dealt to them—a typical human behavior on a cold, dreary winter day; something in winter stirred these feelings up even in the most cheery of creatures. I had pity for them all, but could not help mourn for my own poor circumstance—growing old in a trap. If I had had a spell for each poor soul I looked upon that day, I would have set us all free; I would have given Katiyana her rightful position and identity; each dwarf would have received health and a profound stature; and I would have been anywhere but in a prison. But while I had the power to create spells inside the mirror, my strength and will had grown weak over so many years spent in isolation. Setting myself free had proved impossible; I had tried many times to best the spell the queen had used to trap me inside. It boiled down to the fact that her gift exceeded mine.

It would seem the reflective mood was catching; I sat pondering all of these things with the image of the princess before me. Suddenly, I heard a dreadfully familiar voice.

"What is it that holds your attention so well?"

The coolness of Queen Radiance's tone froze every bone in my body. I quickly cleared my mind so that blankness covered the space between us. She picked up the mirror, which always made me feel dizzy and disoriented. I placed my brow on the inside surface of the glass so that we could talk face to face. "It was nothing," I said, forcing a feigned calmness.

"I don't believe you," said the queen. "Show me what you were just looking at."

"I wasn't looking at anything."

"Liar. I saw what you were looking at. A girl. And there were others."

"Well, all right," I said. I tried to disobey her; I showed her a dozen other girls in a dozen other houses.

"Not that one," she said again and again. "There was a child on the table and a man seated beside him. But there was something different about the man. And there were other different men. And the girl, she looked like . . ."

The queen paused to reflect, and I could only imagine what was going on behind those cruel, black eyes. All of a sudden, her eyebrows rose in an expression of incredulous outrage. "It can't be," she gasped. "Show me the girl!"

I continued to flash images of every girl and cottage I could think of, every one I had seen or learned of over the years.

"I'm going to give you one more chance to live," she intoned.

To be honest, death—while not entirely appealing—was not as horrible to me as the queen knowing Katiyana was alive and well. But I could not allow the queen to kill me. Staying alive was the only way I could hope to protect the princess, to keep watch over her. If I died, the queen could climb inside the mirror and see for herself anyway. So I thought once again of Princess Katiyana and her seven little men.

Jalb had begun chopping potatoes and turnips.

"I'll give you a thousand gold coins if you can stand on your heads," Pokole squeaked to Corto and Arrapato.

"You don't have a single gold coin, let alone a thousand," said Kapos.

"The girl is the richest of us all and she doesn't have a single gold coin either," said Duan.

"Who are they?" the queen demanded.

Then Katiyana spoke. "I'm only rich because I have all of you," she said, laughing. "What would I do without you?"

"The way she talks," the queen muttered. "Her smile and laugh. Those blue eyes."

Maybe I would have to tell her eventually, but I was going to prolong it as long as possible.

"Tell me it's not her," she whispered.

"It's not her," I replied, because I've never been one to disobey the queen of Mayhem.

She looked at me with those stern, dark-as-night eyes, the ones that make you want to shrink until you disappear from ever having existed. "Tell me exactly who that girl is."

I'm ashamed to admit I couldn't even contrive a lie; my mind had gone blank with the shock of discovery. What else was I to do? "It is your daughter, Queen Radiance, the one and only princess of Mayhem."

The silence that followed surprised and frightened me to the core. What would become of Princess Katiyana now? What would become of me?

Queen Radiance sat down, breathing rapidly but deliberately. I'd never seen her in such a state of shock. Or was it rage?

"Where is she?" Queen Radiance finally asked.

"In Fluttering Forest, on the Mischief side. Not too far from Mischief Market, I believe."

More silence.

"You lied to me," she said with a far-off look in her eye. She seemed shocked and distracted.

My mind raced, trying to think of a way out of this, trying to come up with some way to distract the queen, protect the princess, anything. I wanted to crawl out of my skin in desperation.

"You can lie to me."

The pain of betrayal writhed across her face, but when you're a lying, murdering queen, what do you expect?

"I thought you couldn't lie to me."

I mumbled under my breath about how she never trusted me and I didn't know how she could be so surprised. I hoped she'd be so distraught about the lying she'd forget all about the princess.

"And the princess lives? Still?"

"She does." I had wanted to say no, but my secret was out.

The queen leaned in to the glass, so close I thought our noses might touch. She glared into my eyes, our bodies separated only by a thin pane of glass. From my point of view, her skin took on a golden yellow hue.

"I can't kill you yet." Her voice was soft but heavily laced with malice. "I still need you. But rest assured, I will kill you the moment she's dead."

An icy shiver vibrated down my spine as the queen rose, regal and murderous, and glided determinedly out of the room.

Oh, the helplessness I felt then! I longed to call for help. I cried in frustration. I attempted to create spell after spell to get out of the mirror. I bruised my hands and arms pounding on the walls, trying to escape by sheer force. Eventually, I fell into my chair, exhausted and downtrodden. I dumped my head into my hands, stifling the desire to scream. Then I remembered the spell I created all those years ago to protect the princess, and a breeze of hope wafted through the tightness of my chest.

I wanted Katiyana to know who she truly was. I wanted her to defeat Queen Radiance and take her place as the rightful queen of Mayhem. Nobody as cruel and insane as Tirnosha had the right to rule. I only had to find a way to keep the princess safe . . . somehow.

A Faithful Servant

Horrified and perversely amused, I realized that what the queen needed at this time was a faithful servant, one who would kill at her command without question. But let's be realistic, when you torture your subjects and burn their homes, loyalty is a little hard to come by. She first stopped at the prison where her guards held captives until they faced their day of "justice."

I watched as she burst through the door. Three men were seated on the stone benches lining the barred cell doors. They jumped to their feet when they saw the queen.

"Queen Radiance," they said together, as if rehearsed, bowing their heads.

The queen looked at each of them, studying their gruff physiques.

"No, you're not quite right for the job, I think."

What a bizarre thing for the queen to say. If not her own guards and executioners, who else would she require to murder her daughter? What awful plan was she devising?

Queen Radiance spun around and stormed out of the room. I watched the men each let out a sigh of relief as they sat back down on their stone benches.

I watched her dash about the castle, sure and determined, but who was she trying to locate? She walked in haste through a corridor brightened by the sun bursting through the cold windows. And as she did, a young man passed her. He carried a slaughtered furry buck upon his shoulder.

"You there," she called, turning and pointing a finger at him. "Halt."

The young man stopped, the weight of the beast bearing down on his back and legs. He twisted around to make eye contact with the woman giving commands.

"Who are you?" she inquired.

The lack of humility in the boy's response surprised me. He did not even attempt to bow or lower his eyes. "Why, I'm your beast carter, Queen Radiance. Unless of course you intend to have me beheaded. Then you'll have to find another."

Lucky for him, the queen ignored his lack of respect. "You are young," she pointed out.

"You must have the best eyesight in all of Mayhem," the boy remarked.

Queen Radiance looked deep into his brown eyes before taking strides in a circle around him, scrutinizing every inch of his physique. His hair rivaled the queen's in blackness, and he wore it combed away from his face, cut to the nape of his neck.

"And you're attractive."

If you can call covered in sweat and blood attractive. I think his baggy shirt must have been white at one time, but patches of dingy yellow and splotches of red—some dried and faded, others fresh—made for the dirtiest shirt I'd ever seen. Black suspenders held up his black trousers, his shirt puffing out at the waist.

"I underestimated you, my good queen. You must have the best eyesight in the entire world."

He laughed at his own joke, the sound ringing and echoing through the corridor. He had a charming smile, the kind that crinkles cheeks and brightens eyes. I hoped the queen would not kill him for his arrogance or sarcasm, but she looked like she might.

Her serious, threatening glare brought him back to reason and sobriety. "If you don't mind, this kill is not light, and I'd like to get it to the kitchen before my knees give out on me."

I wondered at the queen's strategy. What was she doing? A mere beast carter? Surely she wouldn't ask this boy to do her evil bidding. He wasn't even a hunter or an executioner—just a boy who carries meat from the out of doors to the kitchen, barely noticeable in the workings of a kingdom, maybe even pointless.

"When you've deposited the carcass," she said darkly, "make your way to the Northeastern tower. I will have a bath drawn for you and clothing laid out. The moment you're dressed, I'll have one of my maids waiting to escort you to my private bedchamber. There is something I wish to discuss with you."

Still somber, but perhaps suppressing a smirk, the boy began to shuffle away and follow the mysterious orders of Queen Radiance.

❧ ❋ ❧

An icy chill swept through me when I heard a knock at the queen's door. I looked up toward the surface of the mirror, where before my head had been resting against my fisted hands. The boy had come, just as the queen had instructed.

"Come in," she called out from her tall, cherry wood wardrobe, having just changed into something the color of pale purple lilacs. Lace trimmed the bodice in a rectangular shape, as well as the sleeves at the wrist. I wondered if she sought to appear less intimidating, or perhaps more attractive. Who can guess why a woman changes clothing so many times a day?

The boy stepped into the room, and what a transformation! Every layer of dirt had been removed, and his damp hair hung loosely at the sides of his face. His clothing served as the best improvement. He wore a clean, buttoned white shirt and oak colored trousers, clothing that used to be common among nobility, clothing Fredrick might have worn had his family never been stripped of their titles and forced into poverty and servitude. If it hadn't been for his eyes and the insolent smirk on his face, I would never have recognized him. He gazed about the room, taking in the high ceiling, the walls covered in staggered stone and mounted with rows of candles, the luxurious furnishings, and the painting of Queen Radiance that hung above the bed.

Queen Radiance moved to her vanity as he hesitated near the door, showing the first uncertainty I'd seen in him. Queen Radiance stopped, her hand lightly touching the rim of the mirror, but turned to face the boy before speaking. "I must ask you to do something dire, and yet it's absolutely vital. Do you understand?"

He nodded.

"Before I explain your task, what is your name?" she asked.

"Trevor Blevkey, Your Loveliness. I've been a servant to Her Majesty for nearly seven years." While he did not appear to be frightened by her, the questioning look on his face and the closed stance of his body suggested wariness.

Queen Radiance turned around to pick up the mirror.

"Show me the girl," she commanded.

I pretended not to know which girl she referred to and flashed images of several girls, one of them a servant in the next room.

She held the mirror close to her face and whispered sharply. "I told you I would kill you, and that has not changed. But perhaps I will allow you to have a say in how you die if you cooperate with me."

I couldn't argue with that one. I thought of Princess Katiyana, who was working side by side with Jalb.

"Do you see this girl?" Queen Radiance asked, extending her arms out so the mirror faced toward Trevor Blevkey.

"Well, I'm not blind, Your Grace." He reached out as if to touch the mirror.

"What did you say?" the queen asked, a scowl darkening her beautiful face. She pulled the mirror back, tight against her chest. All the movement began to make me a little dizzy.

His carelessness and sarcasm finally began to dissipate as he sensed the seriousness of his current predicament. He straightened, smoothing his expression and his tone into something much closer to respect.

"I mean yes, Your Majesty."

She thrust the mirror toward him again. "This girl escaped punishment and has been living in Mischief, a traitor to her country."

Trevor studied the scene before him, narrowing in on her face. "Well, what did she do?"

"That is not something you need to know." Queen Radiance continued to hold the mirror up. "You only need know that she must be killed."

"Why are you telling me this?"

"I have chosen you to be the one to kill her."

He blinked slowly, the refusal building explosively behind his eyes. But to my surprise, he won the struggle for silence and merely stood there, face attentive.

"Get a good look at her."

A sudden burst of desperate insight flashed through me, and I saw my opportunity. With the mirror's surface out of the queen's murderous view, I began rapidly shifting my focus, flipping through my memories like a stack of old paintings. I thought of the queen trying to drown her daughter, concentrating as hard as I could. Trevor watched with a raised eyebrow, glancing once at the queen. I thought of King Fredrick carrying the baby away on the queen's horse. I thought of Barney next, rocking the princess; Katiyana picking apples; Jeremy saying good-bye; and finally, tearfully, I thought of the young woman back in the little house with the seven little men. They came to life, jovial and affectionate, eating their dinner.

"I don't understand," Trevor began.

In a flash, I shut off the image and pressed my forehead against the glass, smiling gently in an attempt to avoid alarming the boy.

Trevor squinted and moved closer. "Is someone in there?"

I put a finger to my lips, begging him to be quiet. I pulled my face back, focusing my thoughts once again on the princess, and her image filled the glass just as the queen flipped the mirror's surface back to her view.

"What are you doing?" she demanded.

"Exactly what you asked," I answered smoothly.

She glared at me, then held the mirror against her, as if that would keep me from seeing.

"Take your time if you must. Draw her in with your appealing face, extract her smiles and laughter, and when you've earned her trust, kill her." When the boy gave no answer, she continued, narrowing her eyes and tapping her long fingernails against the back of the mirror. "You do not have a choice. Your queen requires it."

"I'll be honored to do as her majesty commands." And finally, in an exaggerated bow, he folded his arm over his middle and lowered his head almost to the floor. His dark hair flopped forward, brushing across the floor.

Although I could see the bow irked her, the queen maintained her icy calm as she placed the mirror back on her vanity table.

"Good," she said. "The girl lives in the heart of Fluttering Forest with seven dwarves. Not too far from Mischief Market." The queen opened one of the vanity drawers and pulled out a tied, black velvet sack that clinked when she shifted it; coins, I suspected.

"For your journey. And you may choose any horse from the stable."

"Thank you, Your Grace."

Trevor reached for the sack of coins, but the queen held onto it a little longer. "Do. Not. Fail." Her ivory face stood immobile, like chiseled mountain stone.

"I understand," he replied. Satisfied, Queen Radiance set the velvet sack into his waiting hands and watched, with a faraway expression, as he strode quickly from the room.

Wasting no time, the boy headed immediately for the stables. But I was jolted out of my vision when I realized that, for the first time in nearly twenty years, Queen Radiance had entered the mirror. Shocked but unafraid, I stood my ground. Hatred writhed across her face, twisting her beautiful features into an ugly mask. I half expected to die then, and thought of the princess, hoping the spell I'd invited to life all those years ago would protect her if I couldn't. But Queen Radiance settled for slapping me hard across the face. Though it seared with pain, I looked her in the eye and forced myself to smile. I wanted her to believe the sting brought me pleasure.

As she stepped back, I brought my thoughts into sharp focus once more and watched Trevor race away from the castle, the straw-colored horse beneath him kicked into a gallop. I wondered if he realized that, fail or succeed, the queen planned to kill him anyway.

❧ ❈ ☙

Trevor Blevkey began his journey as a confident rider, but when a winter storm hurried in, engulfing the light of the sun and intensifying the bite of the frost, he slowed just before hitting a wall of icy snow.

I could barely see the road anymore, or even a few inches beyond the person on whom I focused. Trevor took a scarf from his satchel and wrapped it around as much of his exposed face, head, and neck as possible, the storm swirling around him. Overwhelmed, his horse went berserk, bucking and whining.

Shifting my focus, I was startled to see sunlight pouring through the window in the queen's private bedchamber. There was something very odd going on. Clouds of blackness, as well as a vortex of angry snow, covered Trevor, but in other areas of Fluttering Forest children romped through the snow in their winter boots, the sun shining above them. In Mischief Market, the sun shone. At the home of Kurz and the other dwarves, the sun burned bright on the rooftop, sending a clump of snow sliding down to the ground below.

I stood up from my chair, walked closer to the surface of the mirror, and thought again of Trevor Blevkey. Oh, the excitement I felt then! I would have jumped for joy if my room had not been as small as it was. My spell was working!

Unable to calm his horse, Trevor dismounted and pulled him into a roadside thicket. I hadn't thought it possible, but the storm worsened, becoming violent as if in an attempt to kill Trevor. The wind and snow slammed against him, forcing him to the ground and repeating every time he tried to get up. A fierce gust of wind unwound his scarf and pulled it into the air. As Trevor reached for it, the horse made his escape, bolting into the storm and out of sight. Finally, Trevor yielded. He crawled between the shrubs of the thicket, collapsing against their bare branches, choosing to wait out the storm rather than face it.

Later that night, the queen returned from her journey to shut the mouths of the "traitors" she had seen in the mirror earlier, the two men we had viewed on the road to Mischief. One had escaped, but the other had been tracked down. And when I say the queen had his mouth clasp shut, I'm not exaggerating. Smiling, she forced a soldier in her army to sew the man's lips together with a needle and embroidery thread. Most unpleasant.

I glared at her as she entered the comfort of her room, removed her gloves, and changed into her bedclothes. Such pure evil; the horror of her actions never even fazed her. After brushing her hair—sitting so close to me I could have spit in her face had I not been bound by the powers of the mirror—she leaned forward and asked to see how Trevor fared on his journey. I assure you she had no pity for him as he huddled in the thicket, trying to keep from freezing to death.

"That's what I get for sending a beast carter," said the queen through gritted teeth. Such beautiful teeth she had, when they weren't gritted.

"Actually, that's what you get for sending anyone out in the dead of winter," I answered.

"Shut up," she snapped. "I'll take care of that."

Queen Radiance drew herself up into a regal stance and began to utter a spell.

I will remind you about spells and how they work. Though talented, the queen could not force any words she uttered to come to fruition. Spells decide for themselves whether or not to be birthed and which characteristics spoken from the mouth of their creator to actually embody. For example, the queen's spell to lock me in the mirror worked for that purpose alone; the spell decided not to enforce the request that I be unable to tell lies to her majesty the queen.

Even still, Queen Radiance's gift astounded me. Few of her spells failed to come to life in some form or another. She closed her eyes and spread out her hands, moving her arms away from her body and upward in a dramatic pose, as if a person's stance had anything to do with it. The threat in her voice made me shiver as she began:

"Spring breezes flow
Sun warm the earth
Winter go to sleep."

"That's it?" I said. "That's your all-powerful spell to help that poor boy kill your only daughter?" Did she think the sun would actually come up at night?

"I hate you," she said to me. Then she swirled around, her sheer white, ruffled nightgown and matching robe swaying behind her as she left the room.

A Collision

In the morning, I had to eat my words, for the snow began to melt even before the sun came up, as if it radiated all the way from the other side of the world and up through the ground. Trevor woke to warm horse's breath blowing across his face. He rolled over, damp earth sticking to the clothes Queen Radiance had provided him.

"So you've come back, have you? That was brave—leaving me here alone to die in a brutal storm."

Trevor stood and patted the animal.

"What do you think about the queen of Mayhem?" He peered into the horse's large, glossy eyes.

"What, no answer? Are you afraid of her too? Well, I'm not." Trevor mounted the beast and began the journey to Mischief Market.

Accepting the advice of the queen, Trevor took his time. He kept the horse at a leisurely gallop, pausing well before sundown to rest each night and taking long breaks during the day, in which he attempted to distinguish between edible roots and horrible tasting plants. I marveled that he had no survival skills, and laughed when he spit out a mouthful of green, partially chewed leaves. Would he make it to Mischief without starving to death?

Finally, late in the morning, three whole days after he'd left the private bedchamber of the queen of Mayhem, the distant sound of voices found their way to the boy.

"Do you hear that?" he asked the horse. "I think we've arrived at last."

And sure enough, they suddenly exited the forest, greeted by the road they'd lost long ago, less than a hundred yards from the fringes of Mischief Market.

Few shops remained open through winter—the ones made of brick or logs that could keep a relative amount of heat—but with the warmer weather, a few tents were being set up as well. Trevor purchased a warm loaf of bread and gobbled it up. I can't say I blame him; warm bread cannot compare to the cold roots he'd been forced to eat on his journey. Then he asked where he could get food and lodging for the horse.

"Stable's down the road a ways," the baker said.

"Do you know of a girl that lives with . . ." Why did he hesitate to say it?

"Yes?" the baker asked impatiently.

"That lives with little men? I mean, men that are smaller in height?" He whispered it, and I wondered if he was trying to be secretive or if he was ashamed to mention such poor creatures.

"Oh, sure," replied the baker. "Comes to market regularly when the weather's right. Speaking of weather, what a warm spell we're having lately." He pulled a fresh loaf of bread from the oven, setting it on a small table and stoking the fire. "I'm going to roast in here today." His large belly shook as he turned to face Trevor again.

"Yes," Trevor said, his eyes flinching. "Strange, isn't it? I nearly froze to death in Fluttering Forest the other night and now it feels like spring."

"Well, let's enjoy it while it lasts. I may even get some business today if it stays like this."

As Trevor turned to head for the stables, the baker added, "The girl hasn't been to my shop all winter, but maybe now that things are warming up, she'll start comin' around again."

"Thank you." Trevor led his horse to the stables and paid for a week of food and lodging for the horse.

I worried about what he planned to do. Would he really kill the princess if given the opportunity? He showed lack of fear, but lack of sense as well. I knew Queen Radiance would kill him if he failed. If he had any hope to live, he needed to carry out her orders. She'd told him to take his time, but he seemed so relaxed and careless about the whole thing, like he'd get around to it if he ever felt like it. I hated not knowing what would come of it all. I didn't think I could bear to wait and see.

❧ ✳ ☙

Katiyana came to Mischief Market the following day with Pokole on her hip. They approached a tent where hand-carved wooden wind chimes were sold. Now that warm, gentle spring breezes blew, Katiyana and Pokole had decided that hanging one outside the dwarf house would bring all sorts of fun, including, of course, the griping of Jalb. They whispered to each other about it and laughed as they moved closer and closer to the shop.

And who stood just outside the tent, munching on an apple that most likely came from Barney's orchard? Trevor squinted when he spotted the princess and her precious dwarf, until seemingly recognizing that Pokole was the child from the image I had showed him in the mirror—the child that sat upon the table. He stopped eating the apple and threw it out of sight, turning away from Katiyana and toward the various chimes that hung from the tent ceiling. With an air of forced civility, he asked the shop owner to pull down one of the wind chimes.

"This one?" the shop owner asked.

"Yes, yes," Trevor affirmed, pulling a coin from the black velvet bag he wore tied to his belt. The day before, he'd gotten cleaned up and purchased additional clothing to supplement what the queen had provided. He ate lavishly, and spent a fair amount of time at the pub. It seemed to me he sought to waste time and the queen's money. If I could have placed a bet with someone, I would have guessed he'd fail at his task and be dead as soon as the queen learned of his indulgences. Lucky for him, she kept busy with the affairs of her crumbling kingdom.

Trevor slapped the money into the owner's outstretched palm and grabbed a wind chime carved with birds. Turning rapidly, he appeared to lose his balance and nearly fell, slamming headlong into the princess and her favorite breakable little man.

Katiyana stumbled backward, never losing the firm grip she had on Pokole. The dwarf, however, rubbed his arm and winced in pain.

"I'm so sorry," Trever exclaimed, a little too exaggerated, in my opinion. I suspected his act, just like his apology, had been an intentional way to get the girl's attention.

But Katiyana had eyes only for her companion. "Are you all right, Pokole?" Katiyana asked him anxiously, ignoring the perpetrator entirely in her worried examination of his little frame.

"I think my arm is broken," warbled Pokole, his voice weaker than usual.

"Broken?" Trevor asked. "How could your arm be broken? He sure does talk funny, doesn't he? Don't worry, little man. As soon as you get a little older your voice will deepen." He spoke to Pokole as if he were a small child, and his comments brought only disapproving stares.

"His bones break easily," Katiyana explained. "Sometimes they break just from standing up."

"Are you being serious?" Trevor asked, but Pokole's facial expressions were all the answers he needed. "Can I do something to help you?"

"No, I'd better get him home," Katiyana said, turning away.

"And watch where you're going next time," Pokole wheezed over Katiyana's shoulder between long, painful breaths.

Trevor reached out and gripped Katiyana's arm.

"Let me at least walk you home," he coaxed.

Instantly, my spell began once again to take life, just as it had when the queen sent Trevor after the princess. It must have been resting, sleeping all those years until need of it arose. The princess's arm began to turn white—snow white—at Trevor's touch. The blanching of color spread to her face, which was usually tan, even in the winter, from all the time she spent working outdoors in her uncle's orchard. It made me wonder again if Trevor really could do the job Queen Radiance had asked him to do.

Trevor pulled his arm away. "You're freezing cold," he said.

Ice crystals began to form on Katiyana's eyebrows.

Pokole reached out to touch them. "You're growing snow on your face."

The princess stared at her pallid arm.

"It's not just your arm," Trevor said. "Your face is the same."

"Are you okay?" Pokole asked.

"Let's go home," Katiyana said, the look of worry barely distinguishable on her colorless face.

Trevor watched her walk away. From behind, she appeared normal: long, dark stringy hair, dress swaying as she walked, child—or rather, little man— in her arms. But from the front, her crystal white skin had only just begun to melt back into its natural color; I could see that the farther she walked away from Trevor Blevkey, the more she looked like herself. I didn't know exactly what my spell was doing, how changing the color of her skin would protect her; at this point, all I knew was that Trevor Blevkey was a danger to the princess.

I let Kat escape from my view as she quickly and carefully exited the market and entered Fluttering

Forest. My focus remained on the boy sent to kill her. He stood there, his feet poised as if considering going after her, until the shop owner interrupted his thoughts.

"Sir, can I help you with anythin' else?" he asked.

Trevor glanced back, irritated. "No. Thank you." He turned his focus back to Katiyana, who could now only just be seen through the thick brush.

"Now that I look at you closer," the man began again. "Have we met before?"

Trevor Blevkey flinched, but otherwise kept his eyes steady on the diminishing target. "No, I don't believe so."

"Prince Iden, is that you?" the shopkeeper asked, tilting his head to the side and scrunching his bushy eyebrows close together.

Whirling, Trevor at last turned and faced the man squarely. "I don't know what you're talking about."

"Don't you remember me?" A beaming smile appeared on the shopkeeper's face as he used all his fingertips to point toward his chest. "I used to work in the castle when you were a child, before the king and queen sent you off for your seven years of servitude. The name's Ryan. Don't you remember? Have you returned to the castle?"

He looked over Trevor's clothes, pausing to scrutinize the thin, braided rope that he used for a belt. "Are you still serving your time? Hasn't it been seven years yet?"

Trevor Blevkey gazed steadily at the man, staring him down with his dark eyes, face expressionless. But I noticed his chest rising and falling heavily beneath his shirt. Was he nervous? At last, he responded in a firm—dare I even say commanding?—tone. "I told you. I don't know what you're talking about."

Undeterred, the man continued on. "No, I'm sure of it. You're taller perhaps, and a bit bulkier, but I'd know that face anywhere. I made some of the toys you played with as a child. I still remember when I came to the castle to construct your new bedroom furniture when you turned ten years old. I'll never forget that—what a privilege and honor to work for the royal family."

A thoughtful expression, tinged in what could only be anxiety, crept over Trevor's face. Or was it Prince Iden?

"I do remember you," he finally said, glancing back over both his shoulders. Was that fear in his eyes? "Can I pay you for your silence?" he murmured, reaching into his pocket.

"Pay me? Silence? What are you talking about?"

Trevor, er, Prince Iden fumbled to open the pouch, his hands trembling furiously. "Nobody can find out," he hissed. "My years of poverty are not up. Not yet. I'm on an errand given from my master, but I could lose the throne forever if my parents suspect that I've left my station."

Only now I remembered a tradition that existed in the kingdom of Mischief. Every boy or girl in line for the throne was expected to leave the royal castle at the age of twelve and live in poverty for seven years. The tradition went back for hundreds of years—generations upon generations. Personally, I think it's a sound idea; it gives the future king or queen a chance to learn what it is like to be poor, thus instilling compassion, thwarting selfishness, and empowering them with the ability to see beyond themselves and their station. This must have been the reasoning behind it all, and it seemed to work; no king or queen of Mischief had ever been as tyrannical as Queen Radiance.

"Now don't fret, Prince Iden. I won't take your money. I can keep a secret."

The prince's wary eyes flicked from the man in front of him to the shoppers nearby and back. "Are you sure?"

"Sure I'm sure. I won't tell a soul."

"You promise?" the boy asked, ducking his head as a group of children ran past the tent. I had only known him as Trevor Blevkey, servant to the queen of Mayhem. Now he was Iden, a prince of Mischief. I tried to let the apparent reality of it all seep in.

"I promise." The man nodded.

A sudden breeze burst through the tent, jiggling the wind chimes in a cacophony of whistles and clinks.

"Is there anything you need? Anything I can do for you, Prince Iden?"

"No. But I'll keep your offer in mind. Thank you."

Iden turned full around, taking one more long look after Katiyana, who had long since disappeared. He meandered away from the tent, carrying the wind chime he'd purchased with the money of his father's enemy.

Iden, Prince of Mischief, a servant in Mayhem— it made me laugh. It must have been a joke. The king and queen of Mischief must have sent him to be a servant in Queen Radiance's castle as a joke, determined to succeed at tricking her without punishment, as long as the queen of Mayhem never found out. I wanted to applaud the king and queen. Oh, the irony! What are the chances this prince would be the servant she chose to kill the princess? Sent to his own kingdom to slaughter the princess of Mayhem? I suddenly felt much better about the whole situation, guessing a prince of Mischief would be far less likely to follow the orders of Queen Radiance than anybody else. And all this time, Queen Radiance's interest in Mischief had encompassed the king and queen and the plans and training of the royal army; I'd never been asked to show her their children— I'd never previously known whether or not they had any. My quiet chuckles turned to laughter; it rang out loud and true as I realized the queen's efforts to have Katiyana killed may soon result in her own ruin.

❧ ✳ ☙

Later, when I had finished wiping away the tears my mirth had brought to my eyes, I began to wonder what on earth would come of it all. How long did Prince Iden think he could evade the queen? Would he continue to try to interact with Katiyana? How would she act toward him after his carelessness with Pokole? Avoiding Queen Radiance for even a month or two would be impossible. I knew she'd come to check on him soon enough. I resolved to watch Iden closely. Time alone could reveal what I wanted to know.

A Princess

Katiyana returned home safely. I watched her wince as Kurz tried to splint Pokole's arm, as if she could feel the pain herself.

"I'm so sorry, Pokole. We should have stayed home today."

"Please don't feel bad. It's not your fault. It's that stupid one's fault."

The other dwarves stood around watching until Kurz couldn't take it any longer. "Would the rest of you get out of here and give us some room to breathe? This isn't as easy as it looks."

"Come on, everyone," Duan said. "It's still nice outside. Let's go for a walk."

"I don't want to go for a walk," Jalb griped. "It's nearly time to start dinner."

Kapos climbed up on a stool where he kneeled

and gave Katiyana a gentle hug and kiss. "He'll be all right, Kat. You'll see."

"Thank you, Kapos."

They all scattered, leaving Kurz to attend to the wound and Katiyana to look on in pain.

"It's not the first time and it won't be the last," Kurz said, an assuring calm in his voice. "Don't trouble yourself about it, you hear?"

"Yeah, I'll be fine," Pokole chimed, bringing a smile at last to Katiyana's face. "But the next time I see that stupid clumsy fellow . . ." Pokole used his good arm to jab at the air.

"Help me hold his arm steady," Kurz said.

Katiyana held Pokole's tiny arm in her gentle hand, her long fingers closing around him. Pokole relaxed in her grasp but jerked when Kurz pulled the linen cloth tightly up over his shoulder.

"Steady now while I tie the knot . . . and there. Good as new."

Jalb came through the door muttering about the cold and how playing a game of stone toss is no fun with Corto and Arrapato cheating all the time. Duan also came in and inspected the wrapping around Pokole's arm.

"Better give it a few weeks," he said.

"And no more going to market," added Kurz.

Both Katiyana and Pokole frowned. Pokole loved going to the market and Katiyana thrived on taking him.

"Now, now," Duan said, trying to sooth their disappointment. "Let's not go feeling sorry for ourselves. It is still winter after all. The snow could return and trap us all in again."

"Yes, wouldn't that be delightful," Jalb muttered.

"There's no need to be upset about not going to market when it's such a rare occasion this time of year anyway," Duan finished.

The others filed in as well. Corto and Arrapato got stuck trying to come in at the same time until Kapos pushed them through the door.

Even with the distraction of all the others, Katiyana focused on her dearest little friend. "I'm so sorry, Pokole."

"Don't be," he squeaked in reply. "They're all twice as nice and helpful when I've got a broken limb." He winked at her.

"Now don't go and get your hopes up of being spoon fed," Kurz said. "That only worked until we learned you could use a fork with your feet."

Pokole shrugged and the rest of them laughed at the little charmer.

Five knocks thudded at the front door.

"Who could that be?" Duan asked.

"Maybe it's seven tiny women looking for love," Arrapato joked.

"Nonsense," Kurz said. "Nobody ever comes into the forest looking for us."

Katiyana looked out the window. "Oh no," she said. Prince Iden stood on the outside. I wondered what he could possibly want until I saw him holding up a wind chime as a peace offering.

"Is it Jeremy Simkins?" Duan asked.

"Enough of all this pointless speculation. Let's just answer the dumb door," Jalb said, beginning a stiff waddle to the front of the house. He opened the door just wide enough to peer outside with one eye. "Who are you?" Jalb asked. "And what do you want?"

Iden tilted his head to one side, trying to get a better view of his inquisitor through the slender crack. "I only came to apologize. I'm to blame for what happened at the market today."

"You forgot to tell me your name," Jalb grunted.

"I'm called Trevor Blevkey."

Duan went to the door. "Come in, come in," he said, bumping Jalb out of the way, their fat rear-ends clashing. He seemed excited that a handsome young man—one not named Simkins—stood outside the door calling on Katiyana.

"Never even heard of the name Blevkey," Jalb muttered after Duan invited the stranger in. "It's probably worse than Simkins."

Iden stepped in, inhaling a deep breath of air as he took in the sight of the tiny house overcrowded with tiny people.

"I've never seen a dwarf before, let alone several in the same room," he announced with glee. "What a spectacle."

Jalb leaned into Duan and whispered, "I hate him already."

"And such a charming old house. Even the vines can't help but come inside." His tone had already switched to mockery. At last he held the wind chime out to Pokole. "I'm sorry, my little friend. Here is something to cheer you up."

Pokole stuck out his tongue and did not accept the gift.

"The only thing that would cheer us up would be for him to leave," Jalb muttered under his breath to Kurz.

"What did you say your name was again?" Duan asked in an effort to distract the prince away from the prevailing rudeness.

"Trevor Blevkey." He clasped his arms behind his back, puffing his chest out.

"Are you all right?" Kapos asked Katiyana. "You look so pale."

Katiyana touched her face, then noticed how white her arms and hands were. "I must not be feeling well. I probably just walked too far today and need rest."

Concerned, the dwarves each crowded around her.

"Maybe you should lie down," Kapos suggested.

"I agree," added Duan.

"You're so cold," Corto said as he and his brother both held on to her arms.

Duan offered to get her a drink and slice of bread and Jalb glared at their guest, as if he suspected the boy brought about the phenomenon. In the center of their anxious eyes and questions, the color in Katiyana's flesh began to return to its normal color.

"Well, maybe I should get going," Prince Iden—disguised as Trevor Blevkey—announced over the hubbub, frowning ever so slightly. I imagine he seldom stopped smiling, even in dire circumstances.

"Yeah, maybe you'd better," Jalb agreed, sending him one last glare.

Iden opened the door, taking a single backward glance at the princess of Mayhem and her little men.

He walked slowly back to the market, ignoring the first signs of spring: buds waiting anxiously to open, birds gathering twigs and leaves to make their nests, bees flying about in search of early flowers. He had the look of someone stuck in the caverns of his own thoughts; how distracted he seemed! His head occasionally slanted to one side as he mumbled indistinguishable one-sided conversation. Suddenly he stopped, staring straight ahead, eyes wide. "She's the princess," he pronounced loud and clear. Iden resumed his amble, talking in an effort to make sense of it. "She's the princess of Mayhem, daughter of Queen Radiance." He grabbed hold of his hair with both hands. "The mirror! That was her in the mirror!"

I wanted to applaud myself, positive my efforts

to show the boy pieces of Katiyana's life through the mirror had been a success. It had worried me that the effects of my spell seemed reserved for whenever Prince Iden came around. But he couldn't murder the princess, now that he knew her true identity. He wouldn't. I felt she was safe again, at least from Prince Iden, who I decided was not nearly as dumb as he looked.

❧ ✳ ☙

Pokole's arm healed slowly. Over the next several days, winter gave a final sigh, cooling the air once more and sending a few helpless flurries from the sky. Then finally, it rested. I believed it had more to do this time with the seasons actually changing rather than the ranting of the queen.

Corto and Arrapato grew restless. And who can blame them? With the temperatures warm enough for Jalb to insist Katiyana no longer cook inside, the princess prepared to take the conjoined dwarf brothers to the market for a performance. In years past, men, women, and children all throughout the village would stop to watch their miniature antics.

"I still think we should try one of our magic tricks," Corto said as the three walked to the market.

How funny they looked walking in synchronized strides. Even Katiyana stepped in unison with them.

"Nonsense," said Arrapato. "We haven't had enough practice yet."

"Well, how about the juggling then?"

"Nonsense, brother. Nobody wants to see two people juggle who can't even stand across a room from each other."

"We could just throw our objects up high in the air. That would be something to watch"

"And what if one of us has to jerk to the side to catch a badly thrown juggling object? He'd pull the other one with him so that he couldn't catch the object he was waiting for. Disastrous," Arrapato finished, silencing his brother.

Katiyana strolled along quietly. She hadn't spoken much at all since Pokole's injury. I suspected her gloom had more to do with feelings of sympathy and guilt rather than having to bid winter farewell. I hadn't seen her so forlorn since leaving Barney's, and I hated to watch her sorrow for what had happened.

When they reached the market, Katiyana borrowed a crate from one of her favorite shop owners. Corto and Arrapato sat upon it while Katiyana stood next to them, calling out to all the market goers within reach of her voice.

"Come one, come all, to see the amazing Corto and Arrapato, whose mother died birthing them."

I sensed it took a great deal of effort for her to be charismatic, given her prior solemnity, but she pulled it off.

"Why does she always have to bring that up?" Arrapato asked in a whisper to his twin seated beside him.

"Shhhhh," Corto answered.

People already began to gather around them. "How would it be, stuck to somebody else for your entire life? You think plowing the field is hard? Try it while attached to another. Have trouble sleeping at night? You know nothing of the difficulties of sleep, for Corto and Arrapato cannot move a muscle in their body without disturbing the other."

"Speaking of which," Arrapato began, leaning his head closer to his brother's.

"Shhhhh," Corto said, throwing an elbow into the chest of his twin.

I had watched the act several times in the weeks before the cold kept them from coming. Some days this interaction was deliberate; people paid more to see the two quarreling or trying to hurt each other, as brothers often do. But on this first adventure after a long winter, it appeared the two were sincerely annoyed with one another, and their behavior soon drew a large crowd. Katiyana lifted the shirt of Arrapato, and then the shirt of Corto to prove they actually were stuck, which drew a chorus of *oooooohs* and *ahhhhhhs*.

"Only a grebice for a peek," Katiyana said, taking coins left and right and securing them in the pouch hanging around her neck.

Suddenly, I caught sight of Prince Iden. He had seen Katiyana and her little friends. He watched her from a distance—the girl he now believed was the princess of Mayhem—as the audience formed a line to each get a close up look of the anomaly being presented to them.

"Smile at the nice people," Corto slurred through his teeth, encouraging his brother to put on his show face.

Arrapato turned to look at his brother's profile. "Sometimes I wish you'd keep your mouth shut." He said it in a booming voice, causing an outburst of laughter from those in the first half of the line.

Katiyana forced a grin, peering at the brothers out the corner of her eye.

"I mean it!" Arrapato reinforced. "I am so sick of you telling me what to do all the time."

A look of concern crossed Katiyana's face as Corto turned his head in rebuttal. "I do not tell you what to do all the time. And I'm sick and tired of your smell."

"What smell?"

"Why don't you two show them some of your tricks?" interjected Katiyana, but it was too late. Arrapato slapped his brother across the face. Stunned, Corto stood defenseless while Arrapato twisted as far as he could and put his hands around his brother's neck.

"Let go of me," Corto insisted, trying to loosen

the choke hold. When he failed at getting beneath Arrapato's hands, Corto punched his brother in the eye. How comical they looked, trying to fight when they could barely even face each other.

"Stop," Katiyana urged, trying to break them up. But there would be no breaking them up. They fell backward off the crate and rolled around in the dirt.

Iden had apparently decided to take action. He approached them.

"Here, let me help you," he told the princess. "I'll grab this one's arms. He seems to be the feistiest." He knelt down and pinned Arrapato's arms to the ground.

"No, don't do that. You'll hurt him!"

"Do you have any other ideas?" Iden was now taking some of Corto's blows. "They're going to kill each other if we don't intervene. Help me out."

Katiyana knelt beside Corto, but as she tried to restrain him, his arm flew straight into her nose. She covered it with her hand and moments later blood started to trickle down her arm.

"Now look what you've done," Iden scolded the still grappling dwarves.

Both brothers calmed down to look at their beloved friend.

"Oh, Kat. I'm so sorry," Corto apologized.

"This is all your fault," scolded Arrapato. He spit at his brother, but it landed on Katiyana's arm instead.

"Enough!" yelled Katiyana. "I ought to leave you both here tonight to sleep outside." The crowd stopped their snickers, their jovial faces changing into tense-looking expressions as they all began to dissipate.

"That was some show," Iden remarked, letting go of his captive dwarf and smirking at the princess.

Katiyana glowered at him, still holding her hand over her nose. Her skin paled, but not so drastically as it had on their previous encounters. "What do you want?" she demanded, a look of anger cemented to her face "First you break Pokole's arm. Now I'm bleeding."

"Well, I'm not the one who hit you in the nose, am I?"

How smug Prince Iden sounded, and that arrogant smirk on his face—I wanted to give *him* a bloody nose.

"I really am very sorry about that, Kat." Corto looked up at the princess, timid and remorseful.

"And I'm sorry for spitting." Arrapato tried to get up, but Corto wouldn't budge.

Iden and Katiyana both came to their feet, helping the attached little men off the ground. As Corto and Arrapato dusted themselves off, Iden stole a moment with the princess. "I just wanted to apologize again. For everything. If there is anything I can do for the child . . ."

"Well, there's not," she snapped.

Iden searched his surroundings like a drowning man. What did he think could help him out of his current predicament? His eyes fell on a lavender bush just beginning to blossom. He marched to it, pulling a knife from his boot, and cut off several stems. "Here," he said, offering them to Katiyana. "Place some of the flowers inside his wrappings. It should help with the pain."

Katiyana paused a moment, indecisive, then plucked the flowers from his hand and stormed away, retrieving Corto and Arrapato on her way out of town.

$$\mathcal{O} \; \text{✳} \; \mathcal{C}$$

The lavender did not speed the healing, but over the next two days, it did greatly alleviate Pokole's pain and discomfort.

"Maybe Trevor Blevkey's not so bad after all," Duan said one afternoon as he lingered at the table after a hearty meal of potato and carrot stew.

"Yeah, maybe we should have him for dinner," Jalb said. The ornery look on his face matched his tone.

"That's a great idea," Duan said. "Why don't you go to the market, Kat, and invite him over for dinner?"

Kurz sat by the fire with his arms folded across his chest. "I think Jalb meant we should eat him for dinner."

"I bet he tastes bad," Pokole said. And just as every other time Pokole opened his little mouth, they all laughed.

But Katiyana did not have to go to the market to invite the prince of Mischief for dinner. Iden showed up at their door only a few short hours later.

"Would you like to go for a walk?" Iden asked Katiyana as soon as she answered the door. Her skin paled slightly, and it again caused me worry. I thought of Jeremy Simkins and how Katiyana had always been safe with him; and her skin had always remained its natural olive color—made even darker by constant sun—in his presence. It made me wonder what Iden's intentions really were. Was he capable of killing her, even now he believed her to be royalty?

All of the dwarves waited for her answer. Pokole stuck his tongue out at the prince.

"I guess so," Katiyana said, looking to Kurz. "If it's okay with you."

"You're not the slave, remember?" he said with a tense smile.

Katiyana grabbed a light shawl to wrap around her shoulders and they strode out of the tiny home, prince and princess. As the door closed behind them, splotchy white began to cover Katiyana's arms, face and legs, signifying to me that my spell still considered Iden a threat. This posed a serious problem, since they would now be in the forest alone.

Stormy Weather

Prince Iden wasted no time testing his theory that the girl he'd been commanded to kill was actually the daughter of the woman who wanted her dead.

"What is your name?" he asked as they departed from the safety of Katiyana's seven little men.

"It's Kat." She pulled the shawl tight around her and took in a deep breath, raising her shoulders and then letting them fall back to their normal resting height. Bleak, gray rain clouds gathered above them, and a constant breeze sent Katiyana's hair flapping and swirling about.

"Kat what?"

The princess looked to her inquisitor. "Kat Whyte."

"Whyte?" Iden asked, his signature smirk ever present.

A clap of thunder roared above them, and a feeble rain found its way from the darkening clouds above, which by now completely veiled the sky.

"Yes. Why, is there something wrong with that?" She sounded annoyed, and I can't say I blame her.

Iden shook his head. "No, no. It's just. . . . Well, where are you from? The name Whyte is far more common in Mayhem than in Mischief."

Katiyana hesitated. "I've never been to Mayhem. I live here in the forest with Kurz and the others."

"Kurz?"

"Yes," Katiyana answered. "He's the one with black hair that was sitting by the fire. I bought him as a slave and he invited me to live with him and the other dwarves."

"How long ago was that?" He led their walk with his hands clasped behind his back. I wondered if he still carried a knife in his boot, but I also had the impression he was more interested in finding out about Katiyana than in killing her. His grinning face and carefree manner prevented me from too much worry.

But why the storm? Was it merely a spring rain, or was it my spell brewing in preparation to defend her? Another clap of thunder roared above, and an intense flash of lightning lit the sky, but the rain continued to hold back. I envied them on their stroll, and imagined the smell of fresh air, rain, and damp spruce and pine needles on a bed of moistening twigs and leaves.

Katiyana's pallid face contrasted severely with her dark hair and eyebrows, and her cheeks, which radiated a cherry hue. I wondered what she thought about in those moments of pondering. Perhaps she remembered what Barney had always told her about never telling anyone where she came from. But Katiyana answered anyway, perhaps because Barney had never bothered to give her any reasons. "I've lived here for a few months. Before that I lived on an apple orchard with my uncle."

"And your uncle, was his name Whyte as well?"

Katiyana only nodded as she brought her solemn eyes downward, staring toward the ground below her. Rain water spotted the skirt of her tan-colored dress.

"What is it like living with dwarves?" He sounded disgusted. Mayhem's laws and practices must have left a mark on the prince; he obviously didn't think very highly of such people.

"It's wonderful. It's the best place I've ever lived. They're all so kind to me." Her tone did not match the enthusiasm of her words.

"But they're dwarves."

"Yes, and you're obnoxious." Katiyana halted and faced the boy who dared oppose her little men.

"Your face is so pale."

Katiyana reached up to touch her cheek.

Iden placed a hand on her forearm. "It's like holding an icicle. Why are you so cold? You're wearing a shawl, and it's not terribly cold out here."

"Perhaps you make me sick," she answered callously, stuffing her arm back under her shawl.

"Have I done something to offend you?" he asked.

Katiyana's eyes shot away from him as if she looked for a way to escape. "I can't describe it." She continued to look away as she spoke. "I'm only this color when you're around. I don't feel the cold, even though you say I'm like ice, but I can see how my skin changes and it alarms me."

She pulled out her arm to inspect it, and then swept it back under the protection of her fuzzy, knitted shawl that was just a shade or two darker than her dress.

"Whenever you're around, I'm uneasy somehow."

Finally, her eyes returned to his, wide and fearless. "And I hate to hear you talking poorly of my friends." Some of her color came back in the heat of her words.

"I'm sorry," he said, and he may have actually meant it. "I will try to take some time to get to know your living companions. I'm sure they're as kind as you say."

For once, the smirk was gone from his face, and he straightened his lips and focused solely on the bright blue eyes of the princess of Mayhem.

"And when I say you're pale, what I mean is that your face is so fair—calm and peaceful—and white as snow." He swept his thumb across her cheek. "It's beautiful."

He held his thumb there on her face, softly stroking her frozen cheek. "You're beautiful," he finished. I wanted to gag.

I couldn't tell if the red in her cheeks lingered from her previous anger, or if she blushed at his flattery, but the longer they stood there, the more the color seeped away from her until Katiyana looked more ashen and uncomfortable than ever. I hoped for some distraction—a branch falling off a tree or a scurrying animal—anything to free her from his advances.

"Can you tell me, is your first name short for anything?" Iden asked, lowering his hand from her face and shuffling into a leisurely pace once more.

Katiyana joined him. "No," she responded. Little did she know.

Iden looked at her strolling beside him. "It's not quite right for you, is it?"

"What do you mean?"

"Kat is so childish. And it doesn't suit you."

Katiyana stopped again. "Do you ever say anything pleasant?"

"I'm sorry," Iden returned, smooth as glass. "That's not what I meant. It's too simple for you. You deserve something more. With a surname like Whyte, and how you sometimes blend in with storm clouds . . .”

“What name are you suggesting exactly?”

“Snow.”

The princess reflected for a moment.

“Snow Whyte. Now that suits you. There, now what do you think?”

Piercing loud thunder rolled above them as white lightning flashed and a sheet of torrential rain fell from the sky. In unison, they ran back toward the dwarf house, Katiyana holding her shawl above her head.

When they reached their destination, they bolted through the door, entering the candlelit, fire-warmed abode and shutting out the fierce storm. Katiyana hung up her dripping shawl.

“Could I call on you again?” Iden asked

Jalb stared at the prince with fierce, blood-thirsty eyes. He grunted at the boy’s request.

“You’re not leaving already?” Duan inquired. “It’s pouring out. Why don’t you stay for dinner?”

Iden’s eyes flicked back and forth between the one inviting him to stay and the one who looked like he wanted to kill him. Finally, he settled back on Katiyana. “May I come again?”

“You may come again if you’d like,” the princess said. “But I think I’d rather stay here than go for any more walks. That way you can get to know everyone else, and we won't get stuck out in the rain."

Kurz looked a bit worried as he watched Katiyana as if he suspected "Trevor Blevkey" of something. I was grateful the princess had such caring guardians. "That sounds like a wise idea, Kat."

Iden cleared his throat. I don't blame him for being nervous; Jalb had that affect on me and I was safe inside a mirror. "Well, I'd better be going."

He thanked Duan for the invite, avoided looking in Jalb's general direction, and bid farewell. Katiyana held the door open for him.

"Good-bye, Snow Whyte," he said, pausing in the doorway. He looked like he wanted to say more, but Jalb came up behind them and kicked the door shut.

"What'd you go and do that for?" Kurz asked.

"I don't like him!" Jalb said, excusing his rude behavior. "He gives me the winkles."

"He does seem to have a strange affect on the color of her skin," Kapos noted. "Is everything all right, Kat?"

Katiyana's color was beginning to come back already.

"See?" Jalb asked. "Suspicious. And I don't like it. I'm sure Blevkey's a worse name than Simkins. Mark my words, we'll all be sorry if we keep letting him come around."

"Hold your tongue," Duan said kindly. "Can't you see you're disturbing the girl?"

Katiyana sat at the table, solemn and searching. "Don't any of you care what I think?"

All the little men bowed their heads except Pokole, who I'm sure cared what Katiyana thought, but hated Trevor Blevkey just the same.

"Of course we care what you think," Kurz said. "How do you feel about Trevor Blevkey?"

"Well, I don't really know anything about him. But I didn't know anything about any of you when I came through that door," she said, nodding toward the front entrance. "It's not fair if we shun him yet. Even if he does have a big mouth."

"Got that right," Pokole interjected.

"And who's to say anything about his name? Who knows if Blevkey is worse than Simkins?" Here she paused. I wondered how long it'd been since she had last thought of Jeremy. As for me, my opinion of him remained unchanged, since he seemed determined to fail at everything, including coming back for Katiyana.

"I won't slam the door on him anymore," Jalb said repentantly. He looked up and glanced around at everyone else. "Unless you tell me to. Then I'd be happy to oblige."

Katiyana looked at Pokole; it was his opinion she cared about most. But he wouldn't even look at her. He began climbing down the table when Corto and Arrapato got up to help him to the ground. Stiff from sitting there for so long, he limped across the room and leaned against the wall near the fire.

It made me proud to watch Katiyana that day—the way she had stood up to a prince and acted with wisdom in regards to judging character. Not to mention being careful around strange boys. But Iden would come back, and not before he concocted a plan dripping with selfish deceit.

❧ ✳ ☙

Fortune watched over Katiyana, or perhaps it was the blessing of my spell. Queen Radiance had been distracted with a few uprisings in Mayhem over these last several days. When she finally came to ask me whether the beast carter had succeeded in the task she'd given him, I used every possible attempt at diversion.

"Did you know, Queen Radiance, that twelve men are meeting right now to discuss your overthrow?"

"I don't care!" she snapped. "Show me the girl!"

"Did you also know that with the warm weather you so cleverly brought about, several trips have been made by your subjects to the kingdom of Mischief, where they hope to gain help and support from the kingdom in bringing about your ruin?"

"Really?" she asked, before realizing my

distractions were working. "Wait a minute, you're lying, aren't you?"

"Yes," I admitted, but that was a lie; people really were traveling to Mischief to ask for sanctuary or help from the throne to bring Queen Radiance's rule to an end. And I could have shown her those twelve men meeting to discuss her overthrow. Better to let her wonder, I decided.

"Show me the girl or I'll come inside and cut off all your toes!"

I relented, showing her the picture of Katiyana looking gloomily across the room at Pokole.

"Impossible," she said.

"Obviously," I said back.

She glared at me with those menacing dark eyes. "What has that fool been doing?"

"Let's see," I began. "I've seen him talking with the princess, walking with the princess, drinking at the pub, and using your money to sleep in the comfort of Mischief's prime inn and purchase extravagant clothing and food. Oh, and I believe he sold your horse because he couldn't afford to keep it lodged and fed anymore."

She closed her eyes. I wondered how much self-control she exercised in that moment not to scream, or to kill me for that matter. When her eyes opened again, she spoke coolly, evenly. "I'll deal with you later. Right now I have a princess to kill." Her black dress twirled as she spun around, her stately grace disappearing as she rushed out of the room's stone-framed doorway.

I turned my concentration to the outside in hopes of seeing the power of my spell flare once more. My anticipations did not go in vain. A winter storm rushed toward the castle—strong and impenetrable, the near black sky rolling in and dumping a whirl-wind of angry white snow. The queen did not quite make it to her carriage before a blizzard overtook the whole kingdom. That's when I knew my spell was stronger than I had ever imagined.

❧ ❊ ☙

That evening, after a meal of pine nuts and scraps left over from Queen Radiance's supper, including hardened bread covered in strawberry preserves, I watched Iden make his way purposefully to the plat-form—the same one where Katiyana had purchased Kurz. The sky in Mischief glowered down, gray and ominous, but the storm remained at a distance; only a few raindrops fell on the dusty ground.

A chubby man busied himself on the platform, holding a small rocking chair in one hand and a worn stool in the other.

"Juno," Iden called.

I remembered Juno—the man who sold dwarves

into slavery and rubbed shoulders with the mysterious Jeremy Simkins.

"Good day, sir."

"Juno, it's me," Iden whispered. "Look carefully."

Juno dropped the furniture and glanced quickly around as if checking for eavesdroppers.

"I don't know nothing," he said, loud enough for any passers-by to hear.

Iden looked around as well, but everyone was busy packing up their shops for the evening.

"Juno, don't pretend not to know me."

Juno came close and crouched down until his head sat just above Iden's. "I can't claim to know you. Not here. I'll lose my position if I help you."

"I'm not asking for help. Just for information."

"What are you doing in Mischief? I thought you'd been assigned somewhere in Mayhem. Must have hated your parents for that."

"Yes," Iden agreed. "Awful place. How is the royal family?"

"All well, as far as I know, but I can't say anythin' more than that." He held up his hands, shaking them as if begging Iden not to ask any more questions.

"It's okay, Juno, old friend. I only wanted to ask you about the princess of Mayhem."

"Prince Iden, you know as well as I do that there is no princess of Mayhem. She died." Juno tried to straighten his fat knees and stand up again. With great effort, he succeeded but had to shake his legs a moment to loosen them up.

Iden leaned forward in anxious excitement. "But where did she die? When? How?"

"When she was a babe, I think. Long ago. I don't exactly remember how. Somethin' to do with wild animals. Her crazy father's fault, the rumor says."

It was true, I reflected. A faulty rumor did exist. Queen Radiance had started it herself. She'd even sent a letter to the king and queen of Mischief, hoping for some gift as an expression of sympathy. The king and queen sent her a rooster with a note that said, "A jester for her Majesty, the Queen of Mayhem, to keep her company now that her family is lost." Queen Radiance sent an army to deprive the kingdom of Mischief its entire stock of poultry. Nonetheless, everyone believed it was Fredrick who had been the cause of the princess's death. But listen to me go on. The princess wasn't dead!

"What was her name?" Iden asked.

Juno turned away from the conversation to collect the furniture once more, but searched his memory out loud in the process. "Katarine . . . Katja . . . Katiyana! That's it. Katiyana." He carried the furniture down the steps that led to the area below the platform, resurfacing moments later. He lowered the floor door and pulled a ring of keys from his pants pocket to lock it.

"I think she's alive."

"Don't be ridiculous, Prince . . ." He interrupted

his own sentence. "I can't call you that. Not here, it's too risky. Is there somethin' else I can call you?"

"My name's been Trevor Blevkey for the last seven years, but listen to me. I'm telling you, she's alive! And I'm going to marry her. I'm going to marry her and be the king of both Mischief and Mayhem."

"If your parents heard you going on . . ."

"Don't worry about that. I'm here because the queen of Mayhem sent me. That's where my handler stationed me—as a servant to Queen Radiance. I haven't left my position, not really." He grew more annoyed with every word. "Besides, what do you care?"

"Fact is, I don't care. It's just I don't want to get caught talkin' to you." He looked around again. "You've got to get out of here, and don't try to talk to me again."

He turned to leave, but Iden called him back. "Now what do you want?"

"Well, I'm out of money. The queen gave me a little, but she had me leave in such a hurry that I didn't have a chance to get any more. I haven't really got a place to stay either."

Juno rolled his eyes. "You're going to be the death of me."

"I'll stay hidden," Iden said, directing his eyes to the door in the platform. "It's too cold to sleep outdoors."

"You want to stay here?"

"Juno, please. I'll make it up to you someday, I promise. I only have a little bit of time left before I return as prince."

"Wait a minute. You said the queen sent you here?"

"That's right." Iden gave a single nod.

"Why?"

"Oh, I don't want to alarm you . . ." Iden shook his head and folded his arms, leaning back in a casual stance.

"Tell me if you want to stay with me." Juno stood with his hands on his hips. I knew he wouldn't budge. Iden must have known it too, because he spilled his secret.

He whispered low. "She sent me to kill a girl. The princess."

"I told you, there is no princess."

"Time will tell, my friend. Time will tell." Iden smiled wide.

Juno unlocked the platform door once more, pulling it vertical. "Go on in. Hope you don't mind sleeping with spiders."

"Thank you, Juno." He slapped the large man on the back before descending.

"Stupid boy," Juno muttered, shaking his head and closing the door. "I reckon he hasn't learned a thing in seven years."

Then snow began to fall.

A Gift

I must say it isn't easy watching people make choices that you know will hurt them. If only there had been a way for me to communicate with Katiyana—tell her Trevor Blevkey was a scoundrel of a prince with his own twisted plans. I never wanted her to let him in again. I wanted him to stay away from her. Marry her just so he could rule both kingdoms? I'd have rather seen her marry Jeremy Simkins, who had spent a long, hard, disappointing winter looking for work.

I think Katiyana sought this experience of getting to know "Trevor Blevkey" to prove something to herself, and maybe even her seven little men. While she stood a comfortable woman's height, had beautiful features, and could learn to do anything with little instruction (most things she could even figure out through trial and error), the one area she lacked was interacting with young men. Other than Jeremy, and an occasional apprentice at the market, she knew nothing of them. Naturally, this made me nervous, and this was one thing I didn't want her to learn through trial and error.

The pointed return of winter did not deter Iden from attempting a courtship with Princess Katiyana. He knocked on their door the same night he came up with his horrid plan, the sound faint in the howling wind.

Corto and Arrapato walked around the room to stretch their legs a bit.

"Was that the door?" Corto asked.

"I don't think so," said Arrapato. "I bet the wind just blew something against the house so it sounded like a knock. Who would come out in this weather and at this time of night?"

"I heard it too," confirmed Jalb.

All of them looked to Kurz for approval to open the door. "Let's see who it is," Kurz said. "I've never seen it snow like this my whole life. Maybe somebody got caught in it and needs refuge."

"Or maybe it's somebody wanting to kill us all," Jalb said.

"Don't be silly," Duan added. "People don't knock on doors planning to kill the people inside."

He laughed. And I laughed as well because I actually knew somebody who did that often—Queen Radiance.

Katiyana sat at the table, playing a game with Pokole. Corto shifted his direction toward the door, pulling his brother along beside him. After fighting briefly over who got to answer it, they pulled the door open together.

"Hello," Iden greeted them, his face bright and expectant despite the cold and dark.

"Why's he here?" Pokole asked.

Duan walked over to the door, his large belly leading the way. "Come in, Trevor. Come in out of that cold and wind."

Iden stomped his feet and shook the scarf around his neck. "Hello, everyone," he said, walking through the door. His manners were always so positive, although just a touch condescending, as if everyone should be happy to see him.

Jalb grunted. Everyone else gave a nod, except Pokole, who refused to look at him.

Iden looked at Katiyana. "Hello, Snow Whyte."

Her face had begun to pale, but at his greeting it reddened a bit.

"Hello, Trevor," she answered.

Kapos stood and pulled over a stool for their visitor.

"Have a seat," he said, slapping the prince on the

middle of his back—it looked to be the highest Kapos could reach. "Warm your feet and dry your coat by the fire."

Trying to court a girl while surrounded by so many pairs of eyes would have been too awkward for me; but from what I could see, Iden loved the attention.

"How are all of you?" he asked, looking around the room.

"Surprised by the sudden change in the weather," Duan said, reclaiming his seat close to the resonating heat of the fire.

Jalb came between them all for a moment to add more logs and stoke the blaze.

Iden tried to get Pokole to look at him. "What are you playing up there, little one?"

Any other of the dwarves would have been angered by the comment, but I suppose Pokole was used to being called things like that. Katiyana searched her little friend's face, hopefully waiting for an answer. Finally, she answered for him.

"We're playing a game that Pokole invented. We each have a pile of sticks and take turns adding them to create a picture."

The show of emotion in her face had dissipated, and it now looked the same color as the whir of white out the window.

"That's a clever game, Pokole. You are a wonder

of a little man," Iden flattered. "How is your arm?" Perhaps Iden wasn't completely unfeeling; it sounded like he really did want to know. Then again, he could have been an actor if fortune hadn't handed him a place in the world as a prince.

Pokole finally looked at his interrogator. "The lavender helps," he said.

"I'm glad to hear it," Iden said, and then turned his attention back to Katiyana.

"And how are you, Snow Whyte?"

"Why does he keep calling her that?" Jalb mumbled, now finished with his chores and taking a seat amongst the others.

Apparently, I wasn't the only one who heard him.

"Do you mind me calling you that, Kat?" Iden questioned.

Red and pink began seeping into her face once more.

"It's not my name," she said, not really answering the question. "And I'm fine. Anxiously awaiting spring."

"As are we all," Duan said, nodding. "Kapos and I can't wait to get back into the garden. Think of all the lovely vegetables we'll eat again."

Katiyana avoided Iden's gaze as she turned to Pokole.

"I need to make some bread for tomorrow since we ate the last loaf at supper. Would you like to help me?"

Pokole glanced at Iden and then shook his head.

"Are you sure? We could spare a little flour to throw at each other."

Pokole shook his head again.

"Kapos, would you see if Pokole would like someone else to play with while I make bread?" Katiyana asked.

Kapos slapped his legs and stood. "Anything for fresh bread," he said.

"May I be of assistance, Snow Whyte?" Iden asked. "I've always wanted to learn how to make bread."

Jalb rolled his eyes and muttered, "Sure he has," which brought a reprimanding glance from Duan, Kurz, and Katiyana.

"Of course you can help," Katiyana said. Then she looked down at Pokole once more. "I'll save the first slice for you. Will that be all right?"

Pokole nodded.

Katiyana showed Iden how to measure the ingredients and stir without spilling. "Jalb gets after me if I leave a mess on his workspace," she whispered.

"Ah," Iden said. "I'll be careful."

He stirred while Katiyana prepared a slab of stone. She showed him how to knead it until it was smooth as polished rock.

Iden touched her arm, then clasped it gently.

"Do you ever get warm?" he asked.

"I am warm," she replied.

"You can't be. You're cold as ice."

Katiyana flushed; Iden's hand remained encircled about her arm. "I do feel warm, but not as warm as the touch of your hand."

"There," he said. "You've got some color coming back into those cheeks."

Katiyana cleverly pulled away as she reached for the slab of stone covered in flour. She shaped the bread and placed it on top of the slab. Then she lay a thin, ragged linen cloth over the top.

"Now we let it rise," she said. "The longer it rises, the more bread there will be."

"So if we let it rise until tomorrow we'll feast?"

Katiyana laughed. "Not exactly," she said, and truly, her cheeks were redder than I'd ever seen them, though the rest of her remained colorless.

"I brought something for you," Iden said.

"For me?" Interestingly, perhaps instinctively, Katiyana looked across the room at the carved wooden box Jeremy had given her. I can't say what thoughts buzzed inside her female head, but it looked as though she revered the box. And Jeremy's coins had been such a blessing to them all.

Iden reached into the pocket of his trousers and pulled out a large, sparkling red gem that fit nicely in the palm of his hand.

"It's beautiful," Katiyana said. "The color is so

red, even redder than blood. What is it?"

"You don't know what it is?" Jeremy laughed.

Katiyana turned away from the others to keep the exchange hidden.

"I've never seen anything like it," she whispered. "How am I supposed to know what it is?"

"I'm sorry," Iden said. "I thought every girl knew such things."

"I wish you wouldn't laugh at me."

"Again, I'm sorry." He bowed his head toward her. "It's a ruby. I dug it out of a cave that my parents used to take me to when I was a boy."

"And it's for me?" Katiyana asked.

Iden laughed again.

"Yes," he said.

"What am I to do with it?"

Iden placed it in her cold hand and pushed her fingers closed around it. "Keep it. It's more valuable than you could imagine."

"Valuable? You mean I could use it to buy things?"

"I'm sure you could," Iden said, grabbing a few peanuts from the workspace and putting them in his mouth.

"But why are you giving me money? Or something that is worth money?"

"Does there have to be a reason?" He chewed with his mouth open. What terrible manners!

Katiyana's blank stare made me think she still did

not understand. Perhaps his gift confused her, since Jeremy had given her a similar gift after telling her he loved her and wanted to marry her. Perhaps she wondered if Iden loved her and wanted to marry her as well. I knew he wanted to marry her. I also knew he did not love her.

"It's a jewel," Iden said. "It's used to make things beautiful."

"Thank you," said Katiyana. I imagine she didn't know what else to say.

Iden stayed for hours, attempting to woo the princess and win over as many of her seven little men as possible. I'd never seen so much flattery! As all of the men stood around the table taking guesses at what Pokole and Kapos were drawing, the princess hid Iden's jewel in Jeremy's lovely hand-carved box.

Once Iden left, everyone breathed a sigh of relief, even Katiyana.

Jalb went about cleaning up after the bread-making, and everyone else sat in a lengthy silence.

"Was I the only one worried where he'd sleep if he stayed the night?" Pokole asked.

Each of the others laughed at him.

"Oh, Pokole," Katiyana said. "What would we do without you? Winter would be a torment."

Kapos got up off his stool and walked to the window. "Maybe winter's finally bowing out."

The snow had stopped, and silhouetted against the

light of the moon, the trees rested from the demands of the angry wind.

"Well, at least I didn't have to cook for him," Jalb muttered. "It's bad enough that he got a slice of Snow Whyte's bread."

Everyone looked at the pudgy dwarf. "What? I happen to like the name. It's just the boy I can't stand."

"She said she doesn't like it," Kapos defended.

"I never said that," Katiyana said. "I just said it wasn't my name."

"Maybe it could be your altername," Corto said.

"I don't like it," Arrapato said, glaring at his brother. Corto rolled his eyes.

"I've never had an altername before," Katiyana said. A smile came to her face. "Do you remember the altername of that girl in the book we read last fall?"

"I do," Arrapato said. "Chew Chew."

They all laughed, remembering.

"I hope you have better taste in books this year," Jalb said to Katiyana as she prepared the table.

"We need a good altername for Trevor," Kurz said.

"How about Stupid?" Pokole asked.

They all stared at him and then burst out laughing.

"What?" he protested. "It fits."

"Pokole, don't be so rude," Katiyana spurted amid her laughter.

"I've got one," Kurz said. "Prince. Since he walks

and talks like he's so much mightier than the rest of us."

Everybody pondered over the name.

"I don't like that one," Katiyana said. "Let's just stick with Trevor Blevkey. And please don't call me Snow Whyte when he's around. I don't like it when he says it. Please don't encourage him."

"But you're only white as snow when he's around," Kurz pointed out.

"Yeah, what's that all about?" Jalb asked. "Suspicious."

"Indeed," Duan said.

Katiyana looked at her arms that now boasted her usual warm tanned tone, one that blended with the color of the medium oak wood of the table.

"Unexplainable," she said softly.

❧ ✳ ☙

Then blackness; I turned my thoughts elsewhere. With the weather on the mend, I knew Queen Radiance would again be eager to find out what the princess was up to. I thanked the stars above for the blessings of my spell, and turned my thoughts to Jeremy Simkins.

I had watched Jeremy from time to time throughout the winter, always with the same results: he traveled the countryside looking for work, returned home, gave all his money to Cora Simkins and started again the next day. Nothing short of boring and repetitious if you ask me. But not this time.

I checked in on Jeremy and where do you imagine he was? He was being escorted out of the royal castle of Mischief! What had he been doing there? I hated it when I missed such things.

I had never paid much attention to the royal castle of Mischief. Such grand doors. Lit by the torches on either side, they towered over Jeremy and the bearded guard who led him out.

"Have you heard?" the guard whispered, leaning close to Jeremy.

"Heard what?" He sounded annoyed. He didn't have time for rumors; he had the countryside to travel, after all.

"Prince Iden is missing."

"Missing?" Jeremy shook his head. "What do you mean he's missing?"

"Disappeared from his post, or so says his handler. Over in Mayhem where he'd been stationed for his seven years of poverty."

Jeremy mulled it over.

"Gone," the guard reaffirmed.

"There's a reason you're telling me this, isn't there?" Jeremy asked.

"Only that I heard you asking the king and queen

for money. If it's money you want, you'll get it if you find Prince Iden. They're offering ten thousand gold coins!"

"Are you sure?" He clutched the guard's arm— what urgency filled his eyes then!

"Come with me. The king and queen asked me to give you something."

Knowing the king and queen of Mischief, I thought it would be some sort of ruse, but the man led Jeremy down the great grassy hill where the royal castle stood. They entered the stables, and the guard let a mud-colored horse out of his stall.

"A gift from the king and queen, because of your poor circumstances." I guessed the queen and king were showing an ounce of compassion to the poor boy. It must have taken great courage to travel to the castle and approach the king and queen begging for money.

A look of knowing passed between them, as if they shared some secret. I hate knowing looks; why didn't they just say what was on their minds? Moments like that always made me feel so isolated.

Under the starlit sky, Jeremy rode away on the horse, traveling long across the country and returning again to the home of Cora Simkins. I couldn't believe it. What on earth was he doing? He tied the animal up to a tree outside, whispering to it so low that I could not distinguish the words. He entered the still house where everyone slept. The sun would be coming up soon. Would he sell the horse? Give the money to the parents that thought so little of him? Did he remember the girl he'd left? The girl he'd promised he'd return to?

Ruby

Every occupant of the little house in Fluttering Forest slept on the floor, since the only furnishings consisted of the table they all ate on, the table Jalb used to prepare food, and the stools scattered all around. Late at night, when the others were sleeping, Katiyana would pull out the ruby Iden had given her, and peer at it in the moonlight.

Iden came daily now, his smile gleaming brighter than the sun. At first, he could not persuade Katiyana to come for a walk with him. So he subjected himself to being a guest in the little dwarf house. Duan constantly asked him questions. They learned that while originally from Mischief, Trevor Blevkey had spent several years in Mayhem.

"Fascinating," Duan replied.

"Why would you want to go and do a thing like that?" Kurz asked suspiciously.

"Do they eat lots of chicken in Mayhem?" Pokole shrugged when everyone stared at him. "What? We never get to eat chicken. I was just wondering."

Jalb glared intensely at the visitor, and I'm pretty sure he fantasized about chopping up his limbs as he stood chopping potatoes for stew.

At last, Katiyana rewarded Iden's toleration for her little men. After nearly a week of watching him squirm under scrutiny, she agreed to let him walk her to the market.

"I don't want you to go today," Pokole pouted. His arm hurt again and he had come down with a fever on top of everything else.

"Hush now," Katiyana told him in her usual kindness. "You're just upset because you can't come this time. But I'll bring you something from the market. Besides, I have to go today. We'll run out of supplies if the weather turns even one more time."

"Don't forget to take your shawl," Duan said. "It may not be snowing, but the cold bites the bones."

Suddenly, I was distracted from my vision of the dwarves' home. The queen stormed into her bedchamber, startling me profusely. I blinked the image of the princess away, shaking my head. I longed for escape as I heard the clicking of her shoes coming toward me. I wanted to disappear—vanish out of her presence rather than be trapped beneath her magical charms, afraid of her reaction to what I knew she'd see.

She asked what Trevor Blevkey was up to. Of course, I told her that he knew about the princess and was trying to win her over so that he could be the king of Mayhem someday.

"You lie!" she yelled at me, slamming both hands on the vanity and rattling my dwelling. Sometimes her rage frightened me and sometimes I found it down-right comical. This time it was the latter. Perhaps it had something to do with the insane way her eyes bulged as she stared down at me.

"I never lie," I defended with a chuckle. I couldn't help myself; she looked so ridiculous with that angry expression on her face, not to mention the red patches that swelled on her cheeks and the heart shape that formed on her skin between her eyes. What next? Steam coming from her ears?

"He must not have it in him. I'll have to do it myself. I have to do everything myself!"

She wore a simple dress cut from dark gray wool in a way that flattered her impressive figure. She lifted her crown off her head, setting it on the vanity, and released her hair from its tight prison.

"You look lovely," I remarked as she headed toward the door.

"Shut up," she retorted, glancing over her shoulder in my direction.

"Don't you want to take me with you?" I asked. "I could help you along the way if something turns for the worse."

She slammed the heavy door in answer.

I waited in anticipation for a storm to come again, but while the sky darkened and the wind blew, only a few timid flakes fell from the sky. Apparently, my spell could not penetrate the arrival of spring, not nearly enough anyway. My heart beat fast—so fast I feared it would give out—watching her ride toward the princess.

"Oh no," I said over and over and over. I tried again to free myself from the mirror, attempting every spell I could utter, but it was no use. It felt like I was being physically blocked every time I tried to form words into a spell.

Giving up, I peeked in on Katiyana and her loathsome suitor once more.

"And how are you today, Snow Whyte?" Iden asked as they strolled along the path that led to Mischief Market.

Katiyana rolled her eyes. "I really wish you wouldn't call me that."

"I'm sorry, Kat. I keep forgetting. How are you today?"

"I'm well, thank you. And how are you?" I'm no expert, but I knew she wasn't love-struck. She leaned away from him when they spoke, as if she was afraid or maybe just irritated. Then again, maybe he smelled like red wine, or sweat, or the onions in the soup he couldn't get enough of at Mischief Market.

"I'm much better now that I've had a chance to look at you today."

Katiyana rolled her eyes again. "I hate it when you say things like that."

"Why?" he asked, pausing along the path where only a few patches of snow remained.

"Because I never know what to say in return."

Iden suddenly grabbed hold of Katiyana's hand. "Then don't say anything."

He glanced down and then lifted her hand, pressing his lips gently as he kissed the back of it. "I'll keep you warm," he said.

Katiyana pulled her hand away and slipped it under her shawl. "I am warm."

After spending some time investigating the ground, Katiyana spoke again, looking Iden in the eye once more. "I've allowed you to continue to come because I thought it only right and fair to learn more of your character, whether it is good or bad. But after all the time we've spent together . . ."

She peered toward the ground again, as if hoping to find a script.

"What?" Iden questioned.

Katiyana focused on his muddy eyes as she shared her true feelings. "Something about you still makes me uncomfortable. Like I'm standing on the edge of something and about to fall off."

Iden subtly leaned his head toward her.

"Don't worry," he whispered. "I'll catch you."

His lips puckered slightly. Katiyana watched him, looking annoyed at first; I'd never seen her roll her eyes so many times in such a short period. When Iden closed his eyes and leaned in for a kiss, Katiyana abruptly stormed ahead of him. I can't say I blamed her for getting angry, since I knew what it was like when someone refuses to listen to you and keeps pestering you. I won't name any names, but I'm sure you can guess who I'm speaking of.

"What do you plan to get for Pokole?" Iden asked, meandering along behind her. I'm sure he knew by now that the princess always softened when he talked about her little men, especially Pokole.

"I'm not sure yet. Something warm." She turned to face her walking companion, a smidgen of softness back in her voice. "And will you help me find him some more lavender?"

"Of course I will. It's not usually in bloom this early, but with that warm spell we had a few weeks ago, it's plentiful. "

Iden took a few smooth, long strides until their feet came in sync.

"I'm falling in love with you," he spoke, gazing at the side of her face. He could have used a few lessons in how to pull off a good lie.

"And then what happens?" Katiyana stopped again, crossing her arms so the shawl formed a tight "V" across her neck. "You'll leave? You'll ask me to wait for you while you go away to take care of some things?"

"No, of course not," he assured, trying again to get closer without her realizing it. As he inched his feet and leaned toward her, his eyes settled on her mouth. Katiyana remained a statue as he closed in on her and kissed her dry, beet-colored lips. It didn't last long. Perhaps her lack of enthusiasm hurt his pride, forcing him to retreat. Then again, he didn't seem like the kind of boy to give up easily.

"You're so cold," Iden said, pulling away.

"I don't feel cold," Katiyana replied woodenly. I couldn't say how she felt about the kiss; I'd never seen her so emotionless.

"What do you feel?" Iden asked.

"I feel confused." She let out a breath of exasperation. "I don't know what you mean when you say you love me. I don't know if it's sincere—I barely know you."

Prince Iden quickly reassured her. "Of course it's sincere. How can you say something like that?"

"I'm only answering your question."

"Okay, no more questions for now." Such cleverness—smooth as the glass I looked through.

"Can we just get to the market?" Katiyana begged.

"Of course," Iden said.

Once at the market, Iden picked out a parasol for Katiyana, and she purchased a new wool blanket for Pokole—he'd complained so much of being cold the last several days.

I sensed Katiyana wanted nothing that day but to be far away from Iden. She constantly left him behind as he browsed, refused his offer to purchase her a glass of red wine, and looked for every opportunity to converse with someone else. But while she found discomfort in his presence, I knew it was far better than being found by the queen of Mayhem.

A dark cloud took over the sky as the princess of Mayhem and the prince of Mischief walked deep into Fluttering Forest. I had never seen either one of them so silent. They reached Katiyana's current home, and before she could even say good-bye to her escort, Kurz came outside to greet her.

"You need to go home, Trevor." Kurz's curt words halted the footsteps of the approaching prince and princess.

My heart sunk within me; I could tell something was wrong. So could Katiyana. "What's the matter, Kurz?"

"It's Pokole."

"Is there anything I can do to help?" Iden inquired.

"I told you, Trevor Blevkey. You need to go home. Now."

Iden turned to leave but watched the scene over his shoulder until the thick of the forest surrounded him.

"What's wrong with Pokole? Is he worse? Oh, I never should have left today. Has he been asking for me? I brought him a blanket." She tried to make her way past the determined dwarf blocking her entrance.

"He fell off the table while you were out."

"Let me in. Let me see him. He needs me right now." She kept trying to skirt her way around him, but he constantly moved to block her. The blanket and parasol she'd been carrying dropped to the ground.

"He died, Snow Whyte." Kurz sniffed back the tears and looked gravely into Katiyana's worried blue eyes. "His little broken body let go."

"No," Katiyana whispered. She forced her way through the door, knocking Kurz on his back side.

"I'm so sorry, Snow Whyte," Duan sobbed. Katiyana walked deliberately toward the table, the shock and terror evident on her face growing with each of her slow steps.

Kurz watched from his position on the floor as he leaned against the doorframe, seemingly too weak to get up. Tears swelled in his eyes, releasing slowly and steadily one by one. Pokole's body rested on the table, around which the dwarves had gathered. Only Jalb's eyes remained dry. Duan and Kapos made room for Katiyana and she grabbed hold of Pokole's little hand.

At the touch, the tears flowed, slick and free out of her eyes and down her rosy cheeks. I'd never seen such pain, such remorse. What a lovely girl Katiyana truly was.

"I should have stayed with him today," she said. "He would still be alive if I had stayed."

She broke down in sobs, leaning over the frail little body, and soon many little arms surrounded her, bearing her up.

"It's awful what happened," Duan said after a time, his chubby arm barely reaching Katiyana's shoulder. "But you can't blame yourself. It will only bring you greater grief. It's a miracle he lived as long as he did. It's a miracle you even got to know him at all."

"I'll miss his little voice," Corto said.

"And the funny things he said," added Arrapato.

"I'll miss him keeping me company on the table while I cook and wash," Jalb remarked with a far-off look in his eyes.

Kurz rose to his feet, turned away from them all and walked outside. Only minutes passed before the rest heard him sawing and hammering.

"What's he doing out there?" Kapos asked.

Katiyana remained stooped over Pokole's body, holding tight to his tiny hand and touching it to her face.

Jalb walked over and looked out the window. "He's making a casket."

This caused Katiyana to break down with greater force. She lay her head on Pokole's chest and cried with such volume and passion it nearly broke my heart.

"Come away from there," Duan said, tugging at Katiyana's waist.

He succeeded at getting her to sit down. Kapos went outside to help Kurz, and a heavy silence fell over the rest of them, all conversation smothered under the power of their grief. What gloom!

By nightfall, a small, sturdy casket made of chestnut wood waited for its occupant. When Kapos came back inside, Katiyana—who had kept faithful vigil by Pokole's side all afternoon and evening—rummaged through the box Jeremy had given her until she found the ruby from Iden. She carried it outside, pulling the door closed behind her. Stars lit up the clear sky and crickets chirped a lamenting song. The distant sound of an owl's hoot echoed through the darkness.

Kurz had also dug a grave. He sat on a tree stump beside the casket, the shovel sitting beside him.

Katiyana held the ruby out to him. Kurz took the jewel from her hand.

"Could you use this in some way?" she asked. "Could you decorate the box somehow?"

"Where did you get this?" he asked.

Katiyana shrugged. She must not have wanted to mention Trevor Blevkey at such a time, and I can't say I blame her. She bowed her head, avoiding Kurz's question altogether.

"Of course I can," Kurz finally answered. "I'll carve a spot in the center of the lid for it to rest."

Katiyana's lips quivered as she whispered her thanks, and she hurried back inside.

❧ ✳ ☙

The next morning, Katiyana and her six little men arose early, none of them having eaten or slept. Pokole's body had rested on the table all night, his casket on the floor beside him, the blanket Katiyana had purchased the day before covering all but his face.

They all stood around the table once more.

"We'd best get to it," Jalb said. "No matter how unpleasant."

Corto and Arrapato stood at the tiny dwarf's head, lifting his shoulders and protectively cradling him. Kurz and Jalb lifted his feet. They placed him inside his box and each gave him some gesture of good-bye: Katiyana kissed his hand and tucked the wool blanket all around him; Kapos said, "Good-bye friend!"; Corto and Arrapato held their right hands over their hearts; Duan placed a book inside his casket; Kurz gave a great big sniff and then gently rested his hand on Pokole's chest; Jalb placed a bottle of wild raspberry jam next to him.

They lingered in the moment, nobody wanting the finality of this good-bye.

Then a knock sounded at the door—Iden and his horrible timing. Undoubtedly he was growing restless, knowing the queen would be after him.

"I'll bust his teeth for coming here at a time like this," Jalb said.

"It doesn't need to come to that," Duan said. "I'll get the door."

"No, I'll get it," Katiyana spoke, shifting away from everyone else and going to the door.

"Are you all right?" Iden asked upon seeing Katiyana's face. "I was worried about you."

"I don't want to see you anymore."

"What do you mean?"

"I mean, I want you to turn around. Then I want you to walk—I don't even care which direction you go. Keep walking. And I want you to always remember this one thing: you are not welcome here."

Kapos began softly clapping in the background, but Duan nudged him to stop.

Iden huffed. "But I don't understand. Yesterday I told you that I loved you. And I thought you were falling in love with me too."

"People say a lot of things they don't really believe, and they put up with a lot of things they don't really want to," Katiyana explained. "I know now that I don't want to see you anymore."

Kurz came behind her and reached up to place a hand on her shoulder. "Good-bye, Trevor."

They closed the door, letting it shut tight in Iden's face, and then returned to the others.

"Help me with the lid," Kurz said, and Jalb quickly obeyed.

The ruby looked stunning on the top, a tribute to the beauty beneath.

"Let's take it outside, men." Kurz led the way.

Each dwarf lifted his share of weight and Katiyana followed closely behind, carrying a bunch of lavender stems in her hand.

Kapos got down in the hole and helped rest the box on its end. Then he climbed back out and all of them pushed until the whole casket was inside.

Every one of them helped to shovel or push dirt on top. When nothing but a mound of smooth dirt could be seen, Katiyana broke the awful silence. "I need to go home now," she said.

"This is your home," Duan said. "You're always welcome here. We'd love for you to stay forever."

"I know. But I need to see my uncle. I need to see my home." Katiyana lowered her head, as if there was something more she needed to say but didn't quite know how to say it. "I just need to be alone."

Jalb packed her a sack of food.

"I'll be back in a few days," the princess promised.

As she walked out the door that day, I knew the

little dwarf house in Fluttering Forest was about to have its loneliest spell ever.

And I tried to comfort myself. Because Queen Radiance would arrive in the heart of Mischief just as Katiyana walked away from it.

Going Home

Katiyana struggled to hold back her tears as she walked the road from Mischief Market to her uncle's house. I imagine she still blamed herself for Pokole's death. Perhaps she even thought it impossible to face the others at such a time. How I wanted to comfort her then, hold her in my arms, and stroke her long hair.

I could only guess how she felt about returning to Barney. Would he be happy to see her? Or angry? How had the orchard been faring? Would the trees be grown over with far too many branches that hadn't been pruned? Were the animals still alive and cared for? As I thought about it, I realized that I looked forward to seeing Katiyana at the orchard again. Somehow, it is where my memories of her were engrained.

Still, she walked, with no thought of me or my spectrum of emotions and speculations. Her tears stopped as soon as the orchard came into view. I knew she loved her little men, but I could tell she had missed this place. Barney's orchard stood on the most diversely beautiful piece of land in all of Mischief. No wonder she calmed upon seeing it.

The sun barely lit the top of the bluff and would soon stop giving its light to anything around her. The bleating of lambs called out as she approached the house, and she smiled at their sound. She tiptoed up the steps of Barney's house and paused. I wondered if she debated whether to knock or simply walk in as she had always done; perhaps she considered turning around altogether. Then her hand clasped the doorknob.

"Uncle?" she called after walking inside. But a dark stillness pervaded the entire house. She came upon the soiled, ramshackle kitchen, placing her hand over her mouth, suppressing a gasp. Mud and animal dung had been smashed into the floor by Barney's footprints. Bare cupboard shelves stared back at Katiyana, as did spills of sugar, flour, milk, and water. It was obvious he had managed poorly without her.

"Uncle?" she called again. And there he was,

lying on his bed, just an outline under his blanket in the lurking shadows of dusk—cold, still, and dead.

Katiyana gasped, this time covering her whole face with both hands. And I don't blame her; the deaths of two people in one day, two people who had been loved, was too much for anyone to bear. But there were no tears for Barney. Regret and wonder, perhaps a twinge of compassion and lingering love, but no tears. He couldn't have been dead very long, and I'm sure that made her feel worse. Had she come back sooner, he wouldn't have had to spend his last hours and days alone.

Poor Barney.

Katiyana quickly thought of the animals. Such an unselfish girl. Sacks of food stood against the barn walls, evidence that Barney had been to market since Katiyana's disappearance. With a renewed look of determination, she fed the animals, pausing to absently stroke the horse's back. They gratefully munched and pecked in silence. Then the princess grabbed a shovel and began digging a hole in the hard ground, just beside the barn. The bright moon served as her only light.

After several hours, she collapsed, I imagine from fatigue and immense emotional strain.

Perhaps nobody knows better than I how it hurts to watch someone in so much pain and anguish, and not be able to help them. I knew she needed sleep, and I knew the night would grow colder. But sleeping outside was surely a better option than returning to the house where she'd be forced to sleep alone, trapped inside the same space as Barney's dead body. I closed my eyes and attempted to overpower my worries by means of distraction.

❧ ✳ ☙

And what was Jeremy Simkins doing with his little bit of gossip about the missing prince of Mischief? I turned my thoughts to the Simkins home where I found Jeremy packing a bag, again under the watchful eye of Becky.

"Where are you going this time?" she asked.

"This time I'm going far, far away. I'll be gone for several weeks. But there is enough food to last until then—I've worked hard the last few days to make sure." He glanced at the girl as he shoved a shirt into his pack. "You'll eat like a queen while I'm gone."

The girl smiled.

"Are you leaving tonight?" she wondered aloud.

"No, Beck. I'll be leaving early tomorrow morning. I'm just making sure everything is ready so I have plenty of time."

"Are you going to walk?"

"No. I'm going to take the horse the king and queen gave me." Jeremy further tousled the girl's hair.

"Why did they give you the horse? Are you sure you didn't steal it? Denuk and Lief are always stealing things. They told me they wanted to steal your horse, but that Mother wouldn't let them."

"Yes, but remember what I told you?" He looked powerfully into her eyes, as if desperately hoping she understood.

"Yes," she said matter-of-factly. "It isn't right to take something that doesn't belong to you."

"That's right," Jeremy agreed with a look of pride.

"So why did the king and queen give you a horse?"

"I guess they felt sorry for me."

"Are you going back to Mr. Barney's again?"

Sadness came over Jeremy's face. "Yes."

"But I thought you hated Mr. Barney."

Jeremy resumed packing. "I don't hate him. Remembering certain things about him makes me sad."

"Because of the girl?"

"Becky, are you ever going to stop asking questions tonight?"

"Because of the girl?" she persisted.

"Yes, because of the girl. Because of Kat."

"Why?"

"Because he hurt the girl. And I wanted to protect her, but I couldn't because I have to stay here and help you and the others. I tried to help her, but now I don't even know where she is or if she's safe. I'll stop by Barney's to make sure the animals are being fed."

"Do you think she'll be there?"

Jeremy lifted a corner of the blanket on Becky's bed and signaled for her to get in. Becky slid under the thin bed cover and Jeremy folded it over her, making sure it fit snug all around. Then he laid his jacket over the top of her for extra warmth. "I don't know." The reflection of the candle flickered across Becky's brown eyes as he sat beside her for one last moment. "Sometimes I wish I had not encouraged her to leave. I wonder if I did the right thing."

"But you always do the right thing," Becky said.

"Not always, but I try. Sometimes it's hard to know what the right thing is. And I couldn't bear it if I failed Kat."

"Because you love her?" the young child asked.

"Yes, Becky. Because I love her." He kissed her forehead. "Now go to sleep."

"But . . ."

"No more questions. If you wake early, you can see me off. Does that suit you?"

She nodded her head, pulled Jeremy's jacket up to her chin and closed her eyes, after which Jeremy blew out the candle and curled up on the floor.

๑ ❋ ๑

The sun rose and trickled through the orchard branches, kissing Princess Katiyana first on the cheek, and then on her forehead. When she sat up, she seemed surprised to realize the hole was big enough to fit her uncle. The task must have felt insurmountable the night before, and I'm sure she'd been unaware of her progress. With renewed strength of body and mind, she heaved him by the arms from his bed, dragging him with great difficulty across the floor of his house, down the steps, through the dirt and dead grass. Had it not been for his thinness—caused most likely by the lack of having Katiyana to cook for him—I don't think she could have done it alone. She straddled the grave, one foot tilted sideways from walking on the dirt pile, and continued to pull. With beads of sweat covering her forehead, she gave one final yank. His legs dropped inside, and the weight of him nearly pulled the princess down as well. But she let go and watched his body drop to its final crooked resting position. She gave him one last sorrowful look, and then used the shovel to begin covering him up with the earth.

What a shame. I'd been indifferent to Barney for a number of years. But even though he hadn't always been kind, I realized what he had given her: a roof over her head, food to eat, clothing, and most important, protection from her hateful mother. Truly, he deserved some honor, and even though nobody knew it, I was happy to be there with Katiyana.

As she rested beside his grave, my mind flooded with memories of her childhood. Scenes from her whole life flickered inside my head like a tragic play: not that there weren't wonderfully happy moments, but they seemed to mean nothing on such sorrowful days. I couldn't help but wonder how the rest of her life would play out. Would it end in tragedy? Though a real possibility, I tried not to think about it, turning my eyes to the horizon.

Just as Katiyana stood to go inside, a figure on horseback came into view from around the barn. It was Jeremy, but Katiyana had not yet noticed him coming. I was eager to see how this inevitable interaction would play out.

Katiyana climbed the porch steps, and just before reaching the door, she lifted her head, her eyes open wide. Suddenly, she burst through the door and ran into the living area and up the stairs. Her excitement surprised me. What was she doing? Her eyes stared at the bed in her little room, the bed she'd rested in most of her life. She bent forward and jerked the pillow, tossing it out of the way to reveal a book. The book Jeremy had given her the day before he left. I had forgotten all about it.

She thumbed through the pages, only glancing at the words and pastel-colored pictures. Where had Jeremy come across such a book—with watercolor drawings instead of black and white? It must have cost a great deal of money. As she looked, the pages parted wide to reveal a folded piece of paper. Mystified, she lifted and opened it.

Dearest Kat,

I hope that as you read this book, you will come to understand how much you mean to me. My parents used to read it to me when I was a little boy. It is now yours to keep. Forever.

Love always,
Jeremy

With haste, she thrust the pages back until she found the beginning, as if she couldn't wait to find the meaning within. I admit suspense filled me as well. What would the story be about? Katiyana read out loud, walking toward the end of the bed and sitting down.

"There lived a shepherd boy
In a valley green and deep
Where in the sun and rain
He kept a flock of sheep.

He tended them with care
And knew them all by name,
Until one frightful day
A vicious wolfpack came.

The shepherd boy ran out
While drawing his red bow,
To meet the pack of wolves
Releasing arrows slow.

The wolves fell one by one
'Til only two remained.
They snarled and drew back
Then turned to run away.

With all the danger gone,
The boy put down his bow
And comforted the sheep
With music soft and low.

But when the sun went down
And darkness filled the air,
The two remaining wolves
Would leave their empty lair.

Now taken by surprise
In the dark and cool night,
The bow could not be reached
And so the boy did fight.

He fought with reckless fists
But was no equal match.
A desperate cry he gave
'Til help appeared at last.

The men came running out
From village houses warm.
They worked to gather sheep
And led them in a swarm.

Now safe, but damp, from rain
The sheep would wait all night,
Bleating for their shepherd
'Til sun's first golden light.

While all the sheep bore blood,
Not one lamb had been lost,
And under morning's dew
They all could see the cost.

The shepherd boy had died,
His spirit gone above.
He'd given his poor life
Defending those he loved."

Katiyana wiped a tear from her cheek. "Oh, where are you Jeremy?" she whispered. Then she looked out the window and spotted his bewildered face as he stood over Barney's grave.

Fellow Traveler

Katiyana rose from the bed and rushed to the window, where she watched him tie up his horse. Jeremy strode into the barn while Katiyana hurried down the stairs, her light brown linen dress flowing gracefully behind her. Was that a smile creeping across her face? She threw the front door open, taking all the steps at once with a great leap. Jeremy heard her landing in the dirt and poked his head out of the barn just as she rounded the corner of the house. Breathless, she stopped before him.

"Kat?" Did he not recognize her? Perhaps he couldn't believe it. But his wariness soon gave away to a wide, relieved smile.

"Kat, I've been so worried about you." He began to approach her, but a sudden, cautious look in her eyes kept him at a distance.

If ever there was a time to speak! But the girl said nothing.

"Is Barney . . . Is the grave for Barney?"

"Yes," Katiyana finally spoke softly.

I figured that not seeing each other for so long had made them both timid. Was Katiyana angry with him? I couldn't tell. Was Jeremy happy to see her? I don't know. Curse that stupid mirror! It nearly drove me insane watching them stare at each other in total silence.

"Would somebody please say something?" I asked in frustration.

As if he had heard me, Jeremy spoke. "Where have you been?" His voice was heavy with wonder. I could tell he was dying to know.

"Where have I been?" Katiyana threw back at him. "Where have you been?"

"I've been . . . at home."

She kept any anger in check and the sarcasm to a minimum. "At home doing what? Your important things you needed to take care of?"

"Yes, Kat. I've been trying to make a living."

"For who? For yourself?"

"No, Kat. I mean yes. For both of us. For all of us."

"Who do you mean by all?"

"I mean my family. I can't marry you until . . ."

He choked a bit on the word marry, but not because

his feelings had changed. That hopeful, unassuming look in his eye—he felt insecure. Would she reject him now after all this time?

Time to change the subject. "Do you still have plenty of money?" he asked.

"Jeremy Simkins!" She yelled it as if trying to wake him up from a solid slumber. "Yes, I have plenty of money. I never needed your money. I've barely even used any."

"How have you been living then? Oh, Kat, I hope you haven't been wanting for anything." He tried once more to close the distance between them.

"Please don't come any closer."

His boots rustled against the dirt as they halted under her gentle command.

Again with the silence! If I had been there, I would have asked more questions.

Jeremy looked at the old house. "How long have you been at Barney's?"

"Only since last night," she answered slowly. "I came and found him . . ."

"That must have been awful for you, Kat. I'm sorry I wasn't here to help." Such sincerity! Despite his flaws, he was a breath of fresh air compared to Prince Iden. He began inching closer again. "Where have you been staying? Why didn't you talk to Juno as I asked? Couldn't you find him?"

"I found him!" I had never seen her so angry

before. Such bitterness! "I found him and realized you'd sent me to a rogue. Did you know that he sells slaves on that platform?"

All during her lecture, Jeremy continued to sneak his way forward. Katiyana, in her passionate outburst, seemed unaware of his movements.

"I never even spoke to him. Not really. I purchased a dwarf as a slave. And I've been living happily in Fluttering Forest ever since."

"You don't sound happy." Jeremy slipped the words in before she could continue.

"The dwarf I bought lived with six other dwarves, and they let me stay in their home. And I did until . . ." She bowed her head for a few seconds. Was she thinking of Pokole? Looking back at her childhood friend, she continued. "But I am always welcome there. Forever. No matter what. When I return, they'll be waiting for me. It is my home now." The finality of her words made me think she would turn and walk away, but she stood firm.

"I'm so relieved you found a safe place to live, and that you made friends."

"I should probably be returning to them soon."

Jeremy had almost reached her by this point. "And yet, you are still here." He closed the final space between them with care. Just before the tips of his boots touched the toes of her shoes, he stopped, placed his hands on her bare arms, and then, as if handling a delicate sculpture, pulled her to his chest and embraced her.

At first, her stiffness convinced me he was too late, that Katiyana would not accept him. But then she melted into him and returned the affectionate gesture.

"Kat, I'm so sorry," Jeremy whispered. "I know you've been waiting for me and that you were counting on me. Believe me, I tried to find you, and I've been worried sick for you these last months. But deep down I knew you'd be all right. You always were capable of taking care of yourself. I'm so proud of you, Kat. You've done so well."

It was a lovely speech to be sure, but I knew the princess was not convinced.

"Kat, won't you say something?"

Her head rested on his shoulder, her eyes closed, her skin its normal olive tone. Though it lacked the extra tan of working under the summer sun, it was nowhere near the color of snow.

Jeremy placed his hands on her shoulders and pulled himself out of her arms with a gentle push. "Kat . . ."

She opened her eyes and Jeremy saw the glistening tears she was fighting desperately to hold back. "Oh Kat, I've made you cry." He fumbled through his pockets for a handkerchief.

"I don't need a handkerchief," she said when he held the white cloth out to her. "What I need are answers."

Jeremy lowered his eyes, twisting the handkerchief

between his fingers nervously before looking back at her. "Kat, again, I'm so sorry. Sometimes I think it would have been better to just leave things as they were. I'm sorry I ever persuaded you to leave this place. I'm sorry so much has changed between us. I'm sorry that . . ."

"What?" Katiyana asked. "What else are you sorry for?"

"I'm sorry that you don't seem to trust me. It hurts me deeply, but I know I don't deserve any better."

"Why won't you tell me what you're doing? Why is it such a secret?"

"It's not a secret, really. I have to make sure my family is taken care of before I can . . ."

Again he halted, not willing to say "marry" out loud.

"Kat, all I wanted was to keep you safe from your uncle Barney until I could provide for you well enough on my own."

"Jeremy, did you mean what you wrote in that letter? The one inside the book you gave me?"

He moved quickly, placing a hand on her cheek. "Every single word."

"And is it still true?"

"Yes." The answer came unfeigned, with resonating surety.

"Jeremy, I want you to listen to me. Carefully." She clasped both his hands and looked intently into his pure, light-blue eyes. "I care for you as well. Very much. I've ached for you to come back for me. I've thought of you every single day. But I've also learned that I can live happily without you. I can't wait for you forever. I won't."

"Kat, I—"

"If this is about how you still have things to take care of, I don't want to hear it."

"But, Kat, there is one more thing. One more chance to clear myself of my obligations to my family." He was desperate now, knowing her true feelings.

"But Barney is dead! Jeremy, we could live here on the orchard." She quickly bowed her head, possibly ashamed by her forwardness. Her next words confirmed this. "I mean, I could live here. And you could work here. We could care for the apple trees as we've always done. There will be plenty for both of us, and enough to help your family."

"But it would take years to be free of them. Totally free." A gust of wind swept Katiyana's hair upward; the morning sun burned bright. "Kat, I know I've been unfair to you. I just need to do one more thing."

"What is it?"

Jeremy hesitated, as if deciding whether or not to tell her something. Then he revealed what I already knew. "Prince Iden is missing."

"Prince Iden?"

"Yes. Prince Iden. He's the son of the king and queen of Mischief."

"How do you know? What does it even matter?"

"I learned about it just the other day. The king and queen are offering a large reward for the person who finds the prince."

Katiyana was about to argue, but Jeremy persisted.

"It would be enough to satisfy my family. More than enough. I'd be free. Totally free." He rested his forehead on hers.

"Free to do what? Why are you so bound to them? You're not a slave." It reminded me of the words Kurz had so often spoken to her. "Are you?"

"No, I'm not a slave. But I am bound by obligation just the same. I wish I could make you understand—"

Katiyana interrupted his words with a kiss, pressing her lips to his. It took me by surprise, but Jeremy accepted willingly. Did she think she could change his mind with a kiss?

Jeremy finally pulled himself away. "I want so much more for you. Please let me do this one last thing. Let me try. If I fail at this, I will come back and we can live on the orchard. But I have to try."

"Please don't leave me again," Katiyana said.

"Please let me try one last time," Jeremy said.

And they stood there, looking at each other and holding onto one another, each too stubborn to give in or reach a compromise. Finally, Jeremy pried himself away. "Just one last try," he said quickly, before turning toward the barn.

Katiyana followed him in earnest as he untied and

mounted his horse. "Please don't go," she pleaded, holding onto the reins and looking up at Jeremy Simkins.

"I love you," he reminded her as he freed the rope from her hand and kicked the horse into a steadily increasing gallop. Katiyana had to cover her face to keep the dust out of her mouth and eyes.

What disappointment! He'd seen her, and she'd seen him. They'd spoken so many words. Yet, nothing had changed between them. Jeremy rode away, and Katiyana must have been thinking the same things I was, experiencing the same frustration.

But she wasn't stuck inside a mirror. As if able to read my thoughts, she exerted her will. Rather than watch him disappear again, she readied Barney's horse with an obstinate look on her face. I cheered her on as she went after Jeremy Simkins, the boy who found it impossible to explain himself.

৯ ✳ ৶

How the queen fretted when she reached Mischief and couldn't find Iden or the princess. She looked all over the market, and when that turned up nothing she entered the forest. What escaped the queen's attention was that searching Fluttering Forest was no small feat, especially when it had to be done by foot; the forest was not a place for a grand carriage.

Wearing improper shoes and bringing only a witless carriage driver ensured a minimal visit to the neighboring kingdom. She never even came close to the dwarf house. Furious and frustrated, she returned to Mayhem.

A Journey at Last

I find it interesting how destructive a mirror like the one I lived inside can be. It constantly gives people access to the lives and business of others, when one ought just to look at oneself and see what improvements need to take place there. Isn't that why mirrors were created in the first place? Looking in a mirror should be a deeply personal experience in an effort to see what faults are there, not for the purpose of seeing others and how they can all bend to your desires and evil whims. I cursed myself time and time again for ever holding on to the stupid thing and vowed to destroy it if I ever got out. This is what I told Queen Radiance when she got back from her failure of a journey.

"Shut up and show me the girl," she snapped.

Katiyana came into my view, riding along the road to Mayhem.

"Where is she going?" the queen asked.

"I believe she is thirsty and wants a glass of ale from the local pub."

"Stop lying to me!" Queen Radiance was fuming by this point. If she had had any less self-control, the mirror would have broken then and there, for she grabbed hold of several things on top of her vanity and threw them off, first a brush, followed by a bottle of perfume whose false lilac smell had choked me for years, and the mirror she used to actually look at herself. I wondered what would happen if my mirror broke while I was still inside. My father had never told me that. Would I die? Would I be free? Would I be broken into pieces along with the glass? Frankly, I did not want to find out.

"She's going after a boy called Jeremy Simkins."

"Then show me Jeremy Simkins." She rubbed her forehead with her fingers, exhaustion masking the anger still barely audible in her tone.

I came upon Jeremy, still riding along the road to Mayhem, only a few short miles ahead of the princess.

"Where is he going?" she asked. I can't believe after all our years together she still expected me to tell the truth. It's a wonder she continued asking me questions at all.

"It's hard to say, Queen Radiance."

That time she only needed to glare at me before I

gave her a real answer. "He's on his way to Mayhem. He's looking for the servant you ordered to kill your daughter."

"And why is he looking for the beast carter from Mayhem?"

"Your beast carter is not from Mayhem."

She continued to rub her forehead, as if doing so would help collect her thoughts. Or maybe she was just exasperated by my fickleness. "Where, may I ask, is he from?"

"He's Prince Iden, son of the king and queen of Mischief."

"What!" She slammed both her hands on the vanity. I'm convinced that if I hadn't been in the mirror she would have tried to strangle me. As if I had anything to do with Mischief sending a prince to work in the royal castle of Mayhem.

"Oh, they'll pay for this." The queen called for a guard.

"Yes, Queen Radiance, your loveliness." This is what she forced her servants to call her. "What can I do for you?"

"Put the army on alert. Wait until you hear from me again. I have some urgent business. But be ready for an attack on Mischief as soon as I return." She turned back to me. "As for you, you're coming with me."

Finally, some sense. She stuck the mirror inside a

velvet sack that she slung around her shoulder—dark and most unpleasant, but at least I was leaving the castle. I worried for Katiyana and needed a distraction. So I turned my thoughts to other things. What better time to check in on Katiyana's little men?

❧ ✳ ❧

Once the images in the mirror came to life, the darkness surrounding me dissipated, comforting me some as I beheld the glow coming from the glass surface.

"Well, she said she'd be back soon. I'm starting to get worried." Kapos reasoned with Duan as they all sat around a fire. "Where did she say her uncle's house was?"

"It's just straight down the market road, heading south on the way to Mayhem. I'm sure she's fine," Duan said.

"But didn't she once say that her uncle was mean to her?" Kurz asked. "What if he's keeping her there? What if he has hurt her?"

"What if Trevor Blevkey stopped her and kept her from coming back?" Corto asked.

"Maybe Jeremy Simkins was there waiting for her and is trying to convince her to stay," Arrapato said.

"All very good explanations for why she may not be back yet," Duan said.

"All very bad explanations," Jalb corrected.

"So what are we going to do?" Kurz asked.

"What can we do?" asked Duan. "Besides find the orchard and ask the girl ourselves why she's taking so long? All of you need to face the fact that you're being impatient because you miss her."

Five dwarves hung their heads.

"It's just twice as bad that she's gone because of Pokole. But she'll come back. We need to show her some trust and give her the space she asked for."

I loved that the little old dwarf had so much hope. But I knew none of them would be able to help our princess now. It was up to me.

꒐ ❋ ꒐

The queen pulled me out. "Show me Katiyana," she said. Evil woman! How could she even speak her daughter's name when she planned to kill her?

I found the princess still riding on the road to Mayhem, curving around the bend in the road that leads east and straight into the heart of Queen Radiance's territory. Her skin got lighter with every pounding step of the horse's hooves as she came closer to the queen. Closer to me. The queen and I rode west, and if everyone stayed on the same course, our paths would surely cross.

"And the boy."

Just as his image came into view, Jeremy veered south off the road, riding toward a rocky hill in his distance. A gentle but steady snowfall surrounded him, cast out from a gray sky.

"He's headed toward Mayhem Caves. We're not far from there." She shoved me back inside the satchel now hanging from the horse. Such a bumpy ride! I thought I might get sick, but distracted myself by keeping watch over everyone.

Jeremy reached the hill and walked up a trail that led to the highest and largest of the caves. I knew the queen's horse switched directions when I felt a powerful jolt that nearly knocked me off my chair. We were riding after Jeremy. I stood up, the suspense too great to remain seated anyway. Smoke rose up into the sky from the cave, blending in with the colorlessness of the atmosphere.

Queen Radiance pulled the horse to a stop. How uncomfortable I was, being thrown around in that satchel. "You're coming with me," she said as she lifted the bag and threw it over her shoulder. "I want you to see this. In person."

"Does that mean you're letting me out?"

I don't know if she couldn't hear me or if she just ignored me. But since I could hear her loud and clear, I guessed it was the latter.

We reached the top, and judging by how breathless the queen was, the climb had been difficult. She rested at the cave's entrance before making her presence known.

Katiyana stopped at the intersection of the road to Mayhem and the road to the caves. I hoped desperately that she would continue on the road to Mayhem, but she studied the ground and the tracks in the deepening snow before turning and heading toward us. What a joyful meeting we would all have, I thought grimly.

"Is someone there?" Jeremy asked, standing up from the rock on which he'd been seated. I heard his voice both in person and from the surface of the mirror, which created a strange echoing quality as the two sounds layered on top of each other. It was nice to hear his voice for real rather than only through the mirror. It was deeper than I'd realized before and had a quality of honesty.

"It's only me," the queen said as she walked into the cave. The orange flames of a fire stood between us, casting light and monstrous-looking shadows on the intrusive walls of the cave.

"Are you all right? Are you lost?"

"No, I'm not lost." The queen walked toward him, slowly, as if to avoid alarming him. She wore a black dress; how dark she must have looked to him, with her black hair and black eyes. Only her pale face and hands stood out in the dim cave.

"Would you like to share my fire? It's cold out."

"Yes, it is." She continued to walk, rounding the fire, approaching Jeremy, turning sideways and bending slightly as though she intended to sit next to him. He did not look alarmed but leaned away from her slightly. She reached into the satchel and pulled me out.

Jeremy watched with interest, until his look changed to one of painful surprise when Queen Radiance whacked him in the temple with the mirror's heavy gilt frame. Falling back, he landed behind the large rock he'd previously used as a seat. The queen dropped me to the dirt beside him.

"Queen Radiance, stop!" I yelled. "You can't do this!" How my head ached!

She smoothed out her dress. "I should have done this long ago. I tried to do this long ago. And I'm sick of your meddling. As soon as the girl's dead, I'll let you free by killing you. But I want you to see this first. I want you to see her die. I want to show you what you should have really seen all those years ago."

I began muttering spells, or at least trying to.

"You can't create spells in there. Admit it, you're powerless."

A snow drift blew inside the cave, and a large one, too; the fire sputtered and nearly went out. I checked on Katiyana, climbing up to the cave. Blasted by a sudden gust of icy wind, she clung to the side of the hill, glancing fearfully at the sharp cliff below her.

"Here she is!" Queen Radiance sang as the princess finally stumbled into the protection of the cave.

Katiyana shook her head and pulled her shawl closer around her shoulders. "Jeremy?"

"I'm the only one here," the queen said.

"I'm sorry. I don't mean to disturb you, but have you seen a boy? I saw his horse below."

"No, I'm the only one here."

"What about me?" I called. It was a good thing she couldn't reach me then; I couldn't have taken any more jostling. She gritted her teeth at me but could do nothing more.

Unfortunately, the howling wind drowned out my weak voice. Queen Radiance stayed behind the fire as Katiyana was forced further into the cave by a strong gust of icy wind.

I decided waking Jeremy would be the only way to help. The queen had dropped me quite close to him. "Jeremy!" I whispered with as much force as I could muster and prevent the queen from hearing. "Jeremy!"

"Won't you come and sit by the fire?" the queen asked.

Another snow drift blew inside the cave, forcing the princess even closer to her mother. "Well, I can't go back out, not with the weather so fierce." Her words barely escaped her lips with all that wind.

"Kat, get away from her!" I knew that voice. Who do you think stood at the cave entrance looking as though he was covered with frost?

"Trevor, what are you doing here?" Katiyana asked.

Prince Iden! What a shock! He must have followed her. He must have followed her all the way from Pokole's burial. I still wasn't fond of the boy, but I'll admit I'd never been happier to see him; he'd be a distraction if nothing else.

"Well, if it isn't the prince," the queen said.

"Who told you that?" Iden asked.

"Prince? Trevor, who is this woman? What is she talking about? What are you doing here?"

Queen Radiance started to get that look in her eye—the one she got when things weren't going exactly how she'd planned.

Iden looked nervous as well, but he approached Katiyana anyway, as if he wanted her protection as much as he sought to offer his own. Safety in numbers.

"Kat, this is Queen Radiance."

"Queen Radiance? The queen of Mayhem?"

"Yes," Iden confirmed.

"What is she doing here?"

"Jeremy!" I hissed. "Jeremy, wake up!" One more body to fight off the queen would be invaluable. I knew the only weapon she carried was a stout knife. The three youthful bodies could surely overpower her. Killing her would be the only way; otherwise, battling her magic would be another matter entirely.

"Kat, listen to me." Iden hooked his arm with hers and held onto her. "Your name is more than Kat."

"Oh, Trevor," she said, exasperated. "How can you bring up that stupid name Snow Whyte at a time like this?" She tried pulling away from him.

Katiyana was the whitest I'd seen her yet. I looked closely at her arm where Iden hung on and she looked like ice. Literally. It looked as though you could shave layer after layer right off of her.

"Enough," Queen Radiance commanded, soft and cool.

A storm cloud entered the cave, looking as though it had a mind and body of its own; it moved with purpose, circling, swirling, filling every crevice. What would happen to us all? "Jeremy!" I yelled it at full volume now, knowing nobody would hear me over the sound of the wind.

"Kat, she's your mother," Iden blurted over the howling wind.

"My mother . . ."

Katiyana's hair blew about frantically, as if trying to escape the inevitable. It also began to lose its color so that it soon matched her skin. How strange she looked! I worried that the spell would harm her rather than protect her.

Jeremy began to stir. I wanted to kick him! "Jeremy, wake up! It's Kat!"

"Kat?" he muttered before sitting up.

Queen Radiance leaned over, sliding her arm down the side of her body until she reached the bottom of her dress. She pulled the knife from her boot.

"She's your mother," Iden repeated. "You are Katiyana. The one and only princess of Mayhem."

Queen Radiance's boots stomped across the cave floor. Iden cowardly backed away from the queen's forward march, leaving Katiyana wide open. Snow, ice, and wind swirled all around her.

"No!" Jeremy yelled just as Queen Radiance thrust her knife forward.

The furious swirl of storm erupted, blasting everyone to his or her knees, shooting an angry flurry of snow upward and outward. Ice shards cut through the air, causing the occupants of the cave to cover their faces in protection. Snow and wind even came into the mirror, giving me the first real chill I'd felt in almost two decades. After one last high-pitched howl, the wind died, suspending the snow in the air for another moment before it began to fall gently to the cave floor.

Then stillness. And calm. The clouds and storm withdrew, pulling speedily out of the cave. And there, on the ground, rested Katiyana's brown colored linen dress, void of the princess's body.

"Where did she go?" Queen Radiance shrieked. "Where is she?"

Jeremy stood up from behind the rock. "Kat?" He ran toward her.

"Kat?" Iden knelt beside where she had been standing. Then he turned his eyes to Jeremy, the figure he'd previously been unaware of. He raised an eyebrow in curiosity. Only a few wispy clouds remained, taking their time as they retreated out of the cave. Then Iden spoke once more. "Brother? Is that you?"

The Queen's Army

I den, what are you doing here?" Jeremy asked.

I wanted to scream! If they would have just let me out of the mirror I could have helped them all figure it out. I was sick and tired of being ignored! But Jeremy Simkins, Iden's brother? That would make him . . .

"Where did she go?" Queen Radiance demanded.

"What are you doing here?" Iden asked Jeremy, ignoring the queen and standing once again.

"I'm looking for you. I heard you'd gone missing and I wanted the reward money."

"Why on earth would you need the reward money?" Iden asked with a scoff. I was still having a hard time swallowing the idea of the two being brothers; they looked nothing alike.

Jeremy looked down at Katiyana's remains—just a

pile of ice and snow now. With the clouds gone, it would begin melting soon. Most unexpected. I had to get out of that mirror.

"This is all your fault!" Queen Radiance shouted. For once she wasn't blaming me; Iden stood on the other end of her accusations.

"Who's she?" Jeremy asked.

"Queen Radiance, meet Kael," Iden said, swinging his arm and gesturing toward his brother with his hand. "Another prince of Mayhem." Iden patted Kael on the back. "My brother."

They embraced. It must have been so long since they'd seen each other—nearly seven years, when Iden would have first left the royal castle of Mischief.

"You'll both have to die," the queen announced.

Iden released his brother. "And what do you imagine will happen to you if you slaughter two princes of Mischief?"

Queen Radiance surprised me with how long she took to consider the question. "On second thought," she began. "Since the girl is gone. Perhaps I'll just let you go free."

I knew she had something else in mind. It wasn't possible that she would let them go without enacting her revenge.

"Now there's an idea," Iden said.

Kael—it felt so strange to call him that—knelt down beside Katiyana's dress.

Where had she gone? How could I bring her back?

Queen Radiance scooted around them, keeping her back to a wall at all times.

"Keep walking," Iden said, resting his fists on his hips.

"Brother, what should we do?" Kael asked.

Iden eyed the queen until she removed herself from his sight. He then knelt beside his brother. "I don't know. I don't even know what happened."

Suddenly, a great shouting came from outside and the brothers stood to find its source. Just below them stood the entire army of Mayhem.

"What are we to do?" Kael asked. "She's sent her whole army for us!"

But I could see what the army had really come for. The queen's captain, a man she had appointed only recently, straddled his horse and waited to greet the queen after she descended the hill. Now that I looked at him up close, I recognized him as one of the twelve men who had been discussing bringing down the queen that day she wouldn't listen to me. It's a pity she hadn't heeded my warning about them. Perhaps she could have prevented appointing one of them as her captain. I felt the smile form on my lips.

"Queen Radiance," his voice boomed. Another rider came up beside him and held a scroll which he unrolled and held out for the captain to receive. "We hereby charge you with the following crimes: Burning the home of Les Farnsworth. Burning the home of Kilderoy Salvy. Burning the home of Tenser Waller.

Burning the home of Marvin Wilkey. Burning the home of Ernst Bage. Burning the home of Gregor Grahn."

I couldn't believe how long he went on! Burning homes, torturing—each torture method getting a full list for itself—murdering, stealing. The queen stood and listened to it all as one hand held up the side of her dress ever so slightly, as if she planned to run as soon as he finished, maybe even before he finished.

"We hereby sentence you, Queen Radiance, born Tirnosha, queen of the kingdom of Mayhem . . . to death."

"You can't do that," she defended, but several men were already moving in to restrain her. "I'm the queen. You can't charge me with anything."

"It looks like she's going to resist," the captain said. "Hold her steady." The queen closed her eyes and began muttering a spell, moving her lips gently at first, but with greater persistence and volume as the spell went on.

"Power of wind, power of rain
Power of thunder and lightning and hail
Power of swords, power of hate
Power of sickness and evil and fate
Come to me now . . ."

"What's happening?" the captain yelled. It appeared his sword was trying to break free from his grasp. A pitch black, thunderous, monstrous storm cloud began to develop right over their heads.

"Stop her!" I yelled, but nobody heard me. I could hear the wind, not only through the mirror, but the whooshing, whipping sounds entering through the cave as well.

The captain's sword lifted from his hands and into the air, joining the mass of commotion in the sky.

The queen went on.

> "Power of darkness, power of night
> Power of ocean and raging sea . . ."

Just as lightning flashed across the entire sky, the captain quickly pulled out his bow and loaded it with an arrow. It took several shots, given the determined, chaotic wind.

Then it happened. An arrow hit her, then another. What aim! I cheered.

I watched the queen's shocked, disbelieving face, surrounded by beautiful dark ringlets, a trickle of blood falling from her perfect mouth. She hunched forward before dropping to the ground with a thud, arrows snapping. She wore her favorite black dress—quite fitting, don't you agree? It's always nice to wear black when someone dies.

The storm quieted, the clouds dissipated, and the captain's sword fell from the sky, landing on the open ground between the army and the base of the hill. The captain dismounted, retrieved his sword, and stuck the queen straight through. If you're going to do a job, you may as well be thorough.

They loaded her body onto the back of a horse and roped her in place before turning to ride away.

"What just happened?" Kael asked.

"Justice," Iden said. "Justice."

I extended my arm, reaching my hand toward the surface of the mirror, hesitant but hopeful. With the queen dead, I knew my prison would have to release me. I closed my eyes as all the memories of what I'd endured inside the mirror flashed in turn through my mind until WHOOSH! A fierce, brief wind sucked me out of the mirror where I landed on my feet, unsteady on the rocky cave floor.

"Justice indeed." The sound of my own voice boomed now that I was free. Both princes spun quickly, on their guard, eager to see who had just spoken behind them. It felt so good to be out of that mirror!

"Who are you?" Kael asked.

"Me?" I said, as if I needed to; there were only the three of us left in the cave. "I'm Katiyana's father."

Resurrection

ut that's impossible," Iden said. "King Fredrick died years ago."

"I didn't say I was King Fredrick. I'm the girl's real father." I turned to the pile of snow, which continued to swirl about even though the wind had died. I worried it would begin to melt now that the sunlight was coming through the cave entrance. I knelt beside where she had stood only moments before. How could I have come so close? How could I get her back? It would have to be a spell.

But the swirling ice crystals began to meld together again, taking the shape of a human body once more. I watched in awe as fingers formed, legs stretched out, facial features returned and frozen hair grew out past her shoulders and beyond, clumpy with pieces of ice. There she lay, white as snow—including her hair—solid and stiff. I bent down and listened for breath, but there was no breath to be heard.

I glanced up at Iden. His arms were crossed over his chest and he wore a confused look on his face.

"Iden, Kael, help me lift her. I can't think in this cave. I need some fresh air."

I struggled to lift even her head.

"We'll carry her," Kael said as he kindly moved in to take my place. I hobbled up to the opening of the cave, my legs nearly crippled from lack of exercise. How I had waited for this moment! Such joy; I was free! And yet what trepidation—poor Katiyana, I had to bring her back.

A jumble of emotions ran through me. Could I conjure a spell under so much pressure? The sky! The real blue sky! I looked up, taking in all its glory and openness, breathing in deeply the cool, fragrant air.

As we descended the hill—how uneven the ground was, such things I'd forgotten about—Iden and Kael whispered behind me.

"Where did he come from?"

"How does he know our names?"

We reached the bottom. My stiff legs begged to be loosened with a long walk, but Katiyana came first. Katiyana, my daughter, my own flesh and blood—could I bring her back?

Kael and Iden gently placed her on the ground

and backed away after giving each other the strangest looks. What worry could be seen in Kael's eyes. I blocked them out. There I was, alone with my daughter at last. I spoke with the greatest feeling, letting the words fill my soul and roll off my tongue with power and humility. And yet I shook with dread, for no spell had ever been so important to me.

"Thank you, Winter Wind,
For your blessings deep,
For placing Katiyana
In your flawless keep.
Return her now, I beg,
Bring her back to life.
Give her back to me;
Remove from her this plight."

I closed my eyes; I couldn't bear to look. An icy breeze swept across my neck. I listened to the stillness all around me. Her dress rustled. Then finally, she gasped for breath.

I opened my eyes as she began shivering violently, as though she'd been in the coldest place. I felt her arms, her dress, her hair, all colder than ice. "Iden, Kael, help me warm her!"

The three of us surrounded the princess and raised her up. I sat behind her and rubbed her arms. She coughed, throwing herself forward and away from my chest where her head had been resting. Kael held her hand. Iden looked on in pity. Slowly, the color began to come back to her skin and hair.

Finally, she opened her eyes. She saw Iden first. "Trevor Blevkey," she said weakly, her head limp and her lips still quivering. "I thought I told you to never come back."

"Kat?"

The princess turned to see Kael. "Jeremy," she said, slipping away from me and falling into his arms. "I was so cold," she whispered in his ear.

"Everything's going to be all right now." He savored the embrace, squeezing her tight. "And look," he said, at last releasing her from his clutch. "It's the prince of Mischief. I'll be getting that reward money after all." He nodded toward his brother.

Katiyana coughed several times, but afterward began to gain her strength once more. "Trevor? You mean you really are a prince? You're the prince of Mischief?"

"My real name's Iden. And let me introduce you to my little brother, Kael." Iden placed his hand on Kael's back. "Second oldest prince of Mischief."

Katiyana stared hard at her childhood friend for a long time, as if she worked at piecing it all together. It was beginning to make sense to me now. Why he had left the orchard. Why he had urged Katiyana to leave as well. Why he had been at the castle that night. He had been serving his seven years.

"Is it true?" she asked Kael in disbelief.

He nodded. "I'm sorry for all the trouble I've caused you. But I really have always loved you. There just wasn't a lot I could do about it. At the time." He cleared his throat, a hopeful look on his face.

Katiyana looked back and forth at the brothers, shaking her head in disbelief. She settled on Iden, contemplating. Then it was as if something dawned on her. "Is it true what you said in the cave? Am I the princess of Mayhem?"

"Indeed," he answered.

"What?" Kael asked.

"It's true," Iden said. "I figured it out on my own. That's why the queen wanted her dead."

"I don't believe it," Katiyana said. "It seems so impossible." Up to this point she hadn't seen me. I knew the back of her head, every imperfect bend of her hair. But I couldn't wait for her to turn around. I couldn't wait to see her see me.

"But if you're the princess of Mayhem and the queen is now dead . . ." Kael mused.

"That's right," Iden confirmed. "Queen." He winked at his brother.

Kael attempted to let it soak in before speaking again. Finally, someone remembered that I was still there. "There's someone else I want you to meet, Kat." He paused, correcting himself. "I mean, Princess Katiyana," He motioned his hand toward me and we all stood up. She turned, and there, positioned before me, was the face of my daughter. The face that looked so much like my own, it was almost like looking into a mirror.

"Hello," I said timidly. What if she didn't accept me?

"Princess Katiyana, this is your father," Kael said.

"Or so he says," Iden added, the suspicion thick in his voice.

"Just look at them, Iden. Can't you see the resemblance? They look more alike than we do."

"My father?" I could have stood there and listened to her voice forever—her pure, clear, live voice. "Is it true?" she asked, a look of hopeful excitement on her face.

"It is," I answered. "For your whole life the queen kept me captive inside a mirror where I could see all of the outside world, including you. I wasn't sure if you were my daughter at first. Queen Radiance married Fredrick soon after our fling, but watching you grow, seeing your face, hearing the way you speak, those blue eyes . . . I've always loved you, Katiyana. Always."

She covered her mouth with both hands, letting out a joyous laugh, and threw herself into my chest, flinging her arms around my neck. I spun her around twice, and then held her head against me and stroked her dark, wet hair. I would never forget the feel of her hair beneath my fingers—the first meaningful experience since my freedom. All the years I'd spent in the mirror had been worth it for that one moment. I delighted in it, let it fill me until I knew I'd always be content that she lived—that she knew I lived.

Eventually, Iden cleared his throat. He had always been such a pest. "So, now what?"

"What do you mean?" Katiyana asked, lowering herself from our embrace.

"Will the kingdom recognize her as royalty? You saw what they just did to the queen. Is it safe to take her to Mayhem? Will they even believe us?"

"The three of us are witness enough. I'm sure they will welcome their new queen with joy. I think I'd like to hear an explanation from Jeremy Simkins, though. Little got past me, Prince Kael, whilst inside the mirror. What on earth have you been up to these past months?"

He lowered his head, seemingly uncomfortable to have all our attention at once.

"Yes, Jeremy Simkins. Where have you been?" Katiyana echoed with her hands on her hips, her eyes squinted in playful reprimand.

My admiration for him only grew as he shared his story. He had tried to break away from the Simkins family, but Cora wouldn't allow it. She'd been counting on the reward from the king and queen for housing Kael through his seven years of poverty. She threatened to report him, which would have resulted in his denouncement. It was a life-changing sum, and I can't say I blamed her.

Just before learning of Iden's disappearance, he had renounced his right to the throne himself, giving up his title as prince of Mischief so that he could pursue a life with Katiyana. That must have been why I saw him leaving the castle that day. But the problem of Cora Simkins remained. The king and queen told him he was now responsible for paying the Simkins family their promised reward himself. The amount would not change, even if he did not complete the seven years, and Cora had the legal right to hold him to it.

I watched as he shared everything he had been through while Katiyana had lived comfortably with her seven little men. I watched her—for real—as she fell even more in love with him listening to it all, and I gladly gave my consent to the match.

"You did all that for me?" Katiyana asked, a smile lighting up her face.

"And I'd do it all again." I always knew I liked that boy.

Iden cleared his throat once more. "That's all very lovely, isn't it? But what about me? What would you have me do, Queen Katiyana?" I wondered if Prince Iden held a bit of a grudge that he'd failed at winning Katiyana over; never before had I seen him so solemn, so submissive.

"Why should I have any say?" Katiyana asked.

"Now that Queen Radiance is dead, I work for you. And since I'd like to complete my seven years of poverty and be eligible for the throne of Mischief someday, I am at your bidding. At least for the next seven days."

"Are you that close to being finished, Iden?" Kael asked.

Iden gave a proud nod.

"We don't have to go back now, do we?" Katiyana asked. "I'm so nervous! What if they don't like me?"

Having known her so well so long, I gave her the assurance only I could give. "They'll adore you."

"Iden, will you return to Mayhem and prepare them with the news?" Katiyana asked. Such suave delegation!

"I could certainly do that, Queen Katiyana." He smiled at her, as if remembering with fondness all their encounters.

"There is somewhere I'd like to go first." She turned to me, her clear blue eyes a welcome change to the dark ones that had exercised power over me for so long.

"Your little men," I guessed.

She smiled and nodded in answer.

Iden interrupted our tender moment of connection. "And would you all mind returning that horse to Juno?"

He nodded toward all the horses tied up to a tree at the base of the hill. "He used to belong to Queen Radiance. But I'm afraid I sold him to Juno and only borrowed him for this trip." Iden then apologized to the princess, who only laughed.

At Last

We returned Queen Radiance's horse to Juno, who I learned was not only a friend of the royal family of Mischief, but Kael's handler as well. He had been the one to place him with the Simkins' family, the one to give him the name Jeremy Simkins. Kael's horse remained with the man—he looked so much fatter in person—while we began our excursion to visit the tiny dwarf house, and I walked behind Katiyana and Kael through Fluttering Forest. I listened to their young flirtatious chatter just this once, vowing to give them total privacy ever afterward. I had watched too much of their lives already.

"You look beautiful," Kael told her. She truly looked stunning in the new dress we'd just bought her at Mischief Market. It was the same rosy color of the darkest part of a ripe peach, and she glowed in it. And her hair! She looked like such a lady with it all done up by someone who knew what they were doing; Barney had never taught her such things, had never known how.

Katiyana showed her gratitude for Jeremy's comment with a humble smile. "I'm so nervous to see them again."

"How can you be nervous? I'm sure they've missed you terribly."

"I'm sure they have, it's just . . ."

Kael waited patiently for her to finish. "Just what?"

"I'll be the queen of Mayhem. What if they despise me?"

How she loved her little men! I knew she'd be crushed if for some reason they did not accept her as the queen of Mayhem. But given how much they loved her, I knew they would.

"There it is," Katiyana said, pausing in the blossoming forest. I couldn't get enough of the forest smells: pine, bark, damp earth, fragrant spring flowers.

Their home looked so much cozier in person. Kurz chopped wood to the side of the house. He stopped when he caught sight of us.

"Can I help you people? Are you lost?"

"Kurz!"

"Kat? Is that you?"

She ran to him, and when she reached the tree

stump he'd been chopping on, she stooped, caught him under his arms, and lifted him up as if he were a child. So much for being a lady!

"That's enough, that's enough," Kurz prodded, patting Katiyana on the shoulder.

Just then Duan and Kapos came around the house from the garden.

"Kat!" Kapos shouted. Duan waddled faster than I'd ever seen him move to greet her.

Corto and Arrapato came outside. "What's all the ruckus?" Arrapato asked.

Katiyana backed away from the others to get a good look at them.

"Wow, you look like royalty," Corto said.

"What's it all for?" Arrapato asked. "What does it mean?"

"Where's Jalb?" Katiyana asked. "I need you all here before I tell you what has happened."

"I'm here," he announced, coming up behind the twins. "Welcome home, Kat." He winked at her, and she beamed in return.

"Everyone, I'd like you to meet Jeremy Simkins."

"I've had enough of this," Jalb said, turning to retreat into the house. Corto and Arrapato each grabbed one of his sleeves and pulled him back outside.

"But his real name is Kael."

Kurz's eyes widened. "Kael? As in . . . Prince Kael?"

"I'm not a prince anymore," he said, taking a step forward. "But I used to be."

Jalb grunted and turned away. I can't be sure, but I thought I heard him mutter something about princes and Simkins.

"And who's he?" Kurz asked, nodding in my direction.

Katiyana walked back to me and grabbed my hand. I clasped hers with vigor—a hand! I'd missed so many things in the mirror.

"This is my father," she said proudly, her smile vast.

"I didn't know you had a father," Corto said.

She looked up at me, our arms now hooked together. "Neither did I."

"And there's more," Kael chimed.

Jalb rolled his eyes and mumbled something again.

"Kat is to be queen."

"But I thought you said you weren't a prince anymore," Duan reasoned.

"I'm not," he said, looking to Katiyana for approval.

Katiyana let go of me, and I felt the first pang a father feels when his daughter chooses another man over him. She slipped her arm through Kael's. What a match they made; I couldn't wait to see my beautiful grandchildren. "He doesn't need to be a prince. One day soon he'll be married to a queen. He'll be a king."

"What on earth are you talking about?" Kapos asked.

"Kat's real name is Katiyana, the daughter of Queen Radiance. She'll be the queen of Mayhem soon," I explained.

Every dwarf looked as though he might bolt for the door and lock himself inside the safety of his home. But Queen Radiance was no more, and they soon learned of it.

The dwarves invited us inside, and I got to finally taste Jalb's stew, which consisted of the best combination of flavors and smooth, creamy texture I'd ever tasted. We spent the evening playing the most delightful game where everyone quizzed me on my knowledge about them. How shocked Kurz was to realize I knew by heart the song he always sang when he worked outside alone. Katiyana read a story, and we all shared a remembrance of Pokole. A happier time I'd never experienced, not in all my life. At last, everything was as it always should have been.

❧ ✳ ☙

After that, the sands of the hourglass slipped away in such a hurry. Iden took his place again as the prince of Mischief, the next in line for the throne.

Katiyana became queen and Kael her king—her doting husband. Much later in life, when Iden would become king, many harmless practical jokes went back and forth between the kingdoms—Iden always referred to his sister-in-law as Snow Whyte. And in all honesty, her skin never returned fully to its natural olive color.

Corto and Arrapato moved to Mayhem, taking a job in the royal castle as court jesters, where they had every opportunity to entertain. Duan and Kapos agreed to take on Barney's orchard, although they would need taller ladders. Only Kurz and Jalb remained at home, but many joyous reunions took place at the castle, the orchard, or the little house in Fluttering Forest. Not ever wanting to be cooped up again, I traveled throughout both countries and even beyond, but always returned to visit my family.

Kael and Katiyana would have many children. They named their first son Fredrick, after the last king of Mayhem, who gave his life for a child that wasn't even his. And their first daughter they named Kaltza, which, in the language of the forefathers of Mayhem, means . . . Mirror.

Book Club Questions

1. Give your thoughts on Barney. What were his good qualities and his bad? How may have things been different if he had kept his sight?

2. Give your thoughts on Jeremy's bold declaration of love and his desires for Kat to leave her home. Did he do the right thing? Did Kat do the right thing in following his request?

3. Names are important in this book. If you could choose a different name, what would it be? Do you judge people because of their names?

4. What do you think of the idea of royalty living in servitude for seven years? Is it a good idea? Why or why not?

5. If you had a magic mirror, and could see everything and anything, what would you use it for? Do you think Jasper used it too much?

6. Compare Kat's reaction to Jeremy's first leaving with his second. How had she grown throughout the story?

7. Consider what it would be like to be attached to another person as is the case with Corto and Arrapato? Are there any advantages? What things would be difficult or even impossible?

8. Who is your favorite dwarf and why?

9. In your mind, what is the most memorable scene in the book?

10. How is this retelling of Snow Whyte similar to and different from other versions?

About the Author

Melissa has been writing stories since she could hold a pencil in her hand and she has a deformed, calloused finger to prove it. She began twisting fairy tales in the fifth grade when she wrote a story about George of the Jungle making his way to Neverland.

Melissa enjoys writing, making music, reading, baking, and running. She lives with her husband, three daughters, and cat named Matilda. You can visit her online:

Blog: lemoninkwell.blogspot.com
Facebook: www.facebook.com/authormelissalemon